BLOOD TIES

DINERO DE SANGRE BOOK 2

LANA SKY

ACKNOWLEDGMENTS

Thanks so much to everyone who supported this draft along the way, including the many beta readers who provided encouragement! Please keep in mind that this story includes dark, graphic and explicit content matter that is not suitable for readers under the age of 18—or for readers who are uncomfortable with the following subject matter: explicit sex, mentions of sexual abuse, mentions of child abuse, mentions of eating disorders, graphic depictions of violence, and mentions of self-harm.

CHAPTER ONE

*M**r. Jaguar is here.*

Those four words have the effect of a seismic shift —though the destruction seems limited to Domino's once calm mood. Abruptly, he shrugs me off, lunging to his feet, and, within the blink of an eye, he's my cold captor once more.

"Where is he?" he demands of Ines.

She gestures helplessly toward the hall, just as the sound of distant footsteps advances in our direction—several sets to be exact. My breath catches as the first pair echoes off the walls, heavy and solid. Male? The second is softer, trailing behind.

Neither visitor, however, seems to have been invited here with Domino's permission.

Nervous energy flutters between him and Ines—but I don't know if I should be alarmed or relieved. *Finally*, I'll come face to face with this Boogey Man I've been supposedly sold to. A part of me should take some sick glee in seeing Domino so visibly rattled, at least.

But I don't.

"Ada-Maria." Domino cuts his eyes to me, but they're unreadable in the semi-darkness. Only his voice conveys a hint of emotion. "Cover yourself," he growls.

I grapple for a handful of the sheets, but I've barely shrouded my breasts when the footsteps grow louder. Each thud resonates like a morbid drumroll as a man finally appears in the doorway.

Fear pinches my spine, and I sit straighter. He's huge. I have to crane my neck to take him in fully and, if he is Jaguar, I'm disappointed. I expected someone who suits the callous, violent description I've gotten of him so far—someone physically ugly to match their brutal reputation.

Instead, he's as much of a twisted contradiction as my current captor is—beauty and brawn in one intimidating package.

In fact, he and Domino share so many similarities, I assume the latter lied to me when he denied they're brothers. They must be. Both sport dark hair, though this man has his cut short. Instead of a haunting green, his piercing eyes are a deep shade of brown that feeds on the shadows in the room.

Animal comparisons pop into my head. Domino is a tiger, quiet and reclusive, preferring to rely on stealth, but fully capable of making his stand with a fearsome roar when he has to.

This newcomer is a lion—or, perhaps more literally, a jaguar. Bold, his smile alone is dazzling, his gaze piercing, lingering over my chest. "Morning, little brother," he says. His booming voice betrays the hint of an accent. Mexican?

I can't decipher it by the time Domino replies. "Jaguar. You're five days early."

"What are you saying?" Jaguar raises an eyebrow. "*Family* can't just drop by to say hello?"

"You're here unannounced," Domino replies, lacking the same enthusiasm. "I'm sure you brought backup. Ines, why don't you go make sure they're comfortable while we have a chat?"

The woman scurries off, and Jaguar watches her go, his gaze indecipherable.

"You know," he says, returning his attention to Domino. "I thought I'd announce my little visit, but then I had a better idea. Why not come see what little Dom-Dom is hiding with my own two eyes? And now that I've gotten an eyeful of her myself, I'm impressed—" He winks, unconcerned by the way Domino moves to stand in front of me, further obscuring his view. "No wonder you didn't want to share her."

"I was to have a week," Domino snaps. I hate him, and yet his unease drives my own dread, sending my pulse racing as I grip the sheets tighter to myself.

Perhaps he hasn't been exaggerating about what he's hinted of Jaguar?

That he's no savior.

As the thought crosses my mind, the man enters the room fully. If I doubted his identity, he wears a short-sleeved black shirt that exposes his muscular arms—along with the full sleeve tattoo of a familiar feline predator crouching beneath carefully shaded leaves on his left bicep.

The rest of his outfit is simple. His plain dark wash jeans are marred with various spots of grease and grime that remind me of the mechanics my father hired to service the luxury vehicles he kept on his estate. His hands bolster the image, gnarled with scarred knuckles and fingernails sporting hints of dirt beneath them.

I carefully inspect every inch of him that I can, but the longer I put off one glaring realization, the more obvious it becomes. I hate myself for noticing, though why should I? I have no loyalty to the man beside me.

And if I were vain enough to care, Jaguar is just as handsome. His face is remarkably expressive, displaying every observation to cross his mind. Irritation. Amusement. Lust.

His eyes keep coming back to me, drinking in longer glances with each pass.

Until my captor steps forward, putting himself directly in front of me. "What do you want?" he demands.

Seconds pass before Jaguar replies. "Don't be so cranky, Dom-Dom. You can still have your week," he says, and I realize that his extended silence was for deliberate effect. He wanted Domino to watch him watch me.

And not say a damn thing.

Unlike those hours when he'd stand emotionlessly by my father's side, Domino is an array of twitching muscle now, practically lurching on the balls of his feet as if he's physically restraining himself from lunging.

"*But*," Jaguar continues, "I don't want you to get too comfy here, skirting your duties, ignoring your role in the *Guarida*."

Guarida. I file away that term, sure I've heard it uttered before.

"Is that a threat?" Domino asks softly.

Jaguar chuckles. "No. It's a... Let's call it a suggestion. I've decided you need a reminder as to what you're missing." Inclining his head toward the door, he raises his voice, "Baby, get in here."

"Coming!"

It's my turn to lurch forward, barely concealing my disgust at the sound of that low, feminine purr. *No...*

But yes—I smell her before she even saunters into the room, her hair perfectly coifed and styled in a blowout, her outfit pretty much nonexistent. Wrapped in a sheet, I'm dressed more conservatively.

Some things never change, not even after ten damn years. Alexi Rojas is just as beautiful, her perky breasts jiggling as she comes to stand beside Jaguar. Her heavily lined blue eyes sparkle, her glossy lips pursed in a forced grin. It's an act, of course. She's no better at hiding her real emotions than I am. Like a snake, her gaze slithers over Jaguar before darting in my direction.

That single glance conveys all the anger one might suspect from a woman who's made it her mission to fuck every man I interact with.

Even my captors.

The bitch. She's still smiling, seemingly unsurprised by the sight of me, battered and bruised. Considering that she's running her hand down Jaguar's chest, she's been in on their plan from the start.

The shock I feel is too dull to really make an impact, though. Unlike Domino, I never put betrayal past Alexi. I'm just surprised her smile isn't half as wide as I'd assume it would be.

"Hello, Domino," she says huskily. Her eyes lower to his hips, and considering I'm faced with his bare ass, she seems to be enjoying the view from her angle.

"You see?" Laughing, Jaguar pats her head before looping his arm around her tiny waist. He's so strong, that simple gesture nearly takes her off her feet. "Everyone's happy. We're all in for a good, fun time, eh, Dom? Little Lexi-Lex will stay here and party for a few days. You have my permission to wear her the fuck out. Give Ada here a rest, eh?" He winks, but Domino doesn't seem thankful.

"You think I need a babysitter, Jagger?" he asks, his tone dangerously soft.

"No." Jaguar's smile falls, and he shrugs Alexi aside. "I think you need a fucking reminder as to the price you agreed to pay, Domino. You roped me into this mess, and I gladly agreed to help you because that's what brothers do, *si*? But let's not pretend like I couldn't take her right now if I wanted to."

"Is that why you're here?" I can't see Domino's expression from here, but I sense the subtle challenge in his tone.

Jaguar laughs. "I haven't touched her, have I? Have your *week* if it's that important to you. Play your little games and fuck to your heart's content. Just don't forget our bargain, the one *you* initiated. You want out? You buy your 'freedom' with blood. *Adios.*"

With a wave of his hand, he turns on his heel, storming from the room. "Have fun, Lexi-Lex. When you get dressed, Dom-Dom, come find me for a little chat. Don't take long."

I nearly collapse with the force of the sigh that leaves my chest. I must have been holding my breath all that time. Then I remember the woman watching from the doorway and stiffen, meeting her hateful stare.

The last time I saw her as anything other than an enemy was nearly a decade ago, in the aftermath of Pia's disappearance.

"She's missing, Ada! What the hell is wrong with you? Don't you even care?"

Aged ten years, she holds my gaze now for a split second before turning away. "Let's have fun, Domino," she murmurs, sauntering over to him with a familiarity that has me clenching my jaw so hard it aches. Her manicured fingers run down his arm in a gentle caress. "I'm yours until Tuesday—"

"Not now." He bats off the hand she tries to place on his chest. "Get out."

She blinks at his stern tone, but scampers obediently into the hall. I can't help but wonder if she also has had a taste of his temper. His collars. His whip. His cock.

"Don't forget what I told you," Domino warns, turning to face me. He must have snatched the pair of slacks in his hand from the closet. As he tugs them on, his eyes rake over my body, devoid of the hunger he displayed last night. He looks conquering instead. A general, surveying land he's already claimed as his. The way my father would look out at the city of Terra Rodea as he gave his political speeches.

"Nothing he said factors into my arrangement with you," he adds, his voice low and tight. "Don't assume that you leaving here negates what you owe me, Ada-Maria. You are mine until the moment I *choose* to release you."

For a second, I'm not sure if that was a promise. Or a request.

Then I see how his eyes blaze, and I know for sure—it was a threat.

"Why sell me, then?" I croak. "If you still think you own me?"

It's dangerous to play word games and semantics with him. A part of me can't resist anyway. I'm as genuinely curious of the answer as I am terrified by the implications of what he means.

I own you.

"Money and blood are two very different currencies, Ada-Maria." He steps forward, brushing his hand along my cheek. There's no warmth in the motion. It's as chillingly possessive as the way he held me last night, cock buried deep. "I recommend you not forget that. Now get dressed."

He turns for the hall, and I sigh, still clinging to the bedsheet. My stomach lurches at the thought of trying to make it to my room with just this thin slip of material to cover myself with.

Only as he crosses the threshold does Domino call back, "Pick your clothing from my closet. Not yours."

I remain rigid on the edge of the bed. From *his* closet. Does he mean for me to wear his clothing?

Warily, I stand, creeping toward the portion of the room in question. As I open the door, I realize the request wasn't intended to limit my options.

Hanging neatly beside his modest selection of masculine apparel is an array of dresses and other clothing items sized for a woman.

The strangest part is that I can't tell if they all were taken from my closet or newly purchased with my body specifically in mind. The general color scheme is familiar—white, black, and cream—but with a new, bold hue that catches the eye, the same color he made me wear after he whipped me.

Red.

He must have had these brought here recently. Perhaps Ines snuck them in during those twisted moments when he had me on the balcony, naked in the jacuzzi. I wouldn't be surprised if, while buried inside of me, he lorded over the knowledge that he'd soon deploy another method of control, just as damning as his collar.

Fuck him.

Anger seems irrational to feel in lieu of everything else—like terror—but I embrace it fully as I tear through the nearest selection of hangers. Deliberately, I overlook anything remotely feminine and focus only on what I know to be his —the shirts and pants and boxers folded neatly in a built-in chest of drawers.

At random, I pick a gray button-down and a pair of black boxers I have no chance in hell of fitting into properly. It's the principle of the matter.

Unwelcomed visitors aside, my original plan hasn't changed when it comes to Domino Valenciaga. My only means of defeating him lies in trying to seduce him. Unnerve him.

Then stab him.

Stab him.

Stab him—repeatedly with his own knife, all while gazing into his eyes so that he knows I was the one who twisted the blade. Me.

Ada-Maria Lucia Pavalos.

I will have the last laugh. God, I swear I will. Until then, he can lord over my body as he pleases. I won't break.

"You will use this bathroom."

I flinch as his voice drifts from the direction of the bedroom. I find him there, casually lifting our torn, damp clothing from the floor. A grunt of appreciation dies in my throat, and I hate myself for the way my gaze finds the firm curve of his ass.

With his back to me, it's easy to forget the sheer depths of evil this man is capable of. His body is sin, beauty, and strength melded into one glorious form. Flexing muscle dances beneath his skin in a mouth-watering display.

I almost forget I'm meant to despise him.

Then he turns to face me. "Over there." He inclines his head toward the direction of the balcony. "Follow the balcony around to the left."

I bite my lip before obeying, exiting into the warm morning air to find the full extent of the estate unfolding before me. In the dark, what looked like a sheer, endless drop turns out to be a small hill where the terrace gardens meet swaths of rolling, lush fields.

Standing here feels so surreal—bringing home just how isolated we are in this tiny sliver of the world. A man could easily hold a woman captive on a property like this one.

Forever.

Luckily, my stint at Domino's villa already has an end date —Tuesday. By the beginning of next week, I'll belong to Jaguar and be subsequently dragged off to only God knows where.

"I said to the *left*."

I flinch as the reminder is voiced directly against my ear, I didn't even notice him coming up behind me, gripping the railing on either side of my body, trapping me here.

"Don't let the arrival of prying eyes lull you into a false sense of security, Ada-Maria. They won't stop me from punishing your insolence in any way I see fit," he warns, his voice a fraction deeper. "Trust me, I'll very much enjoy having an audience to perform for, their gasps drowning out your screams…"

I shiver, sufficiently cowed. Still, I can't resist a parting jab of my own. "Shouldn't you be busy fucking *her* now?"

Alexi.

Her presence bends the rules of this hellscape prison, and I latch onto the distraction. It's petty to be jealous at a time like this, but fear is the only alternative. It was easier to suffer as a lone captive under a madman's purview. But as a third wheel, forced to inhabit the same dwelling as two of my enemies fuck like rabbits in the other room?

Or plot against me…?

"She can join us, if you'd like," Domino says in a tone so neutral I can't tell if he's joking. "I, however, am not fond of sharing my toys."

I cringe, noting yet another subtle warning. About Jaguar? He's sold me to him, and yet he seems irritated by the reality of what that means.

It's a dangerous theory to test. His possession isn't out of concern for me, of course—mere jealousy. But how strong?

Hopefully strong enough to buy me more time.

"I could ask her what positions my new owner might like." What I intend to sound mocking comes out far too hoarse. I'm horrified. Still, I can't stop. "If he likes anal or oral—"

"Enough." His grated rasp startles me silent as he grabs my arm, manually steering me toward the direction he first indicated. To the left. Just beyond the bedroom doorway is a narrow path leading to a sliding glass door, and inside is a space that might be classified as a bathroom.

Or a torture chamber.

Still, behind me, Domino cups the back of my throat. "This is where you will bathe from now on," he declares against my ear. "And where you will bathe *me*. You can start now. I think we both could use a shower, no?"

He's right. His seed is still drying between my thighs, his taste in my mouth, his sweat on my skin.

And yet, Alexi's presence is too glaring to ignore.

For whatever reason, amid the possibility of being sold and the arrival of Jaguar, *she* stands out as the most alarming factor in this twisted equation.

Why the hell is she here?

"Aren't you going to invite your guest?" I croak, still unable to pull off a playful tone.

He turns, stepping into me so that he's facing me directly, his jawline grazing mine. "Jealousy isn't becoming on you, Ada," he scolds, his tone low with warning. "Don't misunderstand me—you will never mean more to me than as a tool. A body. A hole. Whatever I desire in the given moment—" He cups my cheek, roughly smoothing a stray curl behind my ear as he pulls back to hold my gaze. "If I want another woman, or another man, or several to fuck you—or whatever the hell I want them to do, I will say so. Do you understand?"

My eyes brim with tears as I force a nod.

But I won't let him hurt me without a parting shot in return. Prying my dry lips apart, I croak, "I'll be ready for every last one of them. Jaguar seems like he might be promising in that aspect at least."

His eyes narrow, but he turns away before I can decipher what the reaction might mean. Instead, I shift my focus to examining the room in full, becoming more awed—and terrified—with every observation I make.

It's massive, everything gleaming with a shiny new aura that makes me suspect it's an addition that he had built specifically for this purpose.

To "bathe" together in torturous harmony.

At the back of my mind, that suspicion doesn't mesh with the fact that he plans on selling me by the beginning of next week. Why go through such trouble?

But this man is a mystery I don't have the energy to solve. I'm too damn tired to.

So rather than think, I stare and make a note of every alarming detail of this space. There is an enclosed walk-in shower large enough to constitute an adjacent room, lined with black marble and complete with large, built-in benches on either side. A computerized screen affixed near the entrance presumably controls the spray.

Across from it is an oval-shaped pristine tub, large enough to fit two people—and more. The sleek silver fixtures give it a more clinical design than the other bathroom. A look that implies it could be used for soaking, as well as the perfect vessel for a madman to boil his kidnapped lover alive just for the hell of it.

The thought makes my breath catch in my chest, though I'm not sure which detail unnerves me more. The fact of him actually doing that to me, or that I referred to myself as his lover.

I'm not.

The appraising look he sends my way next makes that more than crystal clear—I am his trophy. A toy. A minor inconvenience.

"Get in." He nods to the shower stall and reaches for his slacks, intending to remove them. I look away, my cheeks flaming.

Not that I have the right to any shred of modesty. I've already seen and experienced nearly every inch of him. What little I haven't lingers in my mind, and I can't resist sneaking another glance at it as he marches past me and fiddles with the shower's electronic screen, his ass bare.

That mark on his chest undermines everything I've come to believe about Domino Valenciaga—before the kidnapping, at least. More than anything he's said or done, the sight of that scarlet, surgical scar proves that the man I knew was a well-crafted lie.

The real man is a stranger. Domino isn't even his name.

He is Navid Inglecias, brother of Pia, the girl who was once my best friend—until she went missing—a disappearance Domino insists was because of my father. That's why he's done all of this, after all, betrayed us and killed my parents.

He thinks Roy Pavalos murdered his sister.

And that I know why.

CHAPTER TWO

"I said get in."

I snap to awareness at his hostile tone, but he doesn't seem inclined to follow up with violence. Yet. He's already gotten the water going and steps beneath the spray first.

Numbly, I set aside the clothing I procured for myself on a nearby row of pristine gray countertops. When I face him again, I'm still wrapped only in a sheet. As the seconds tick by, I take my time fiddling with the twisted fabric to study him in full.

Based on Jaguar's demand, I have until Tuesday. On its face, I'm not even sure what that date symbolizes, or what I plan to do in the meantime. It's not like I have a wealth of options—I could either escape, kill Domino outright, or convince him not to sell me. The sad part? I'm not sure which of those aims is even remotely achievable.

I already tried the first plan to no avail.

Killing him is a far more tempting option.

But seduction… It's the only method I've had even a modicum of success attempting—though, I assume that depends on what one might determine as success. I've gotten him to listen to me, anyway, and let his guard down long enough to sleep in the same bed.

Twice.

That must mean something.

"Don't make me tell you a third time." His voice, aided by the roar of rushing water, comes as a low rasp I know better than to challenge. Without fanfare, I yank the sheet away from my body and stagger toward him, wincing as I walk directly through a cloud of warm steam.

"Wait." He meets me as I cross the threshold, grabbing my wrist. I wince before I realize what he's doing—unhooking a brown watch from my wrist. I've forgotten I'm still wearing it, one of his, taken from his closet.

He throws it onto the counter, near my pile of clothing, and turns his back to me. "Sit—" He nods to indicate a long bench on the other end of the space. The surface is textured so that I have purchase on it, even while wet. Shuddering, I find myself fixated by the only sight in view—him, his naked body facing away from me, his hands braced over the stone wall.

The angle strains the coiled muscle along his back and upper thighs, conveying better than words how this morning's impromptu visit has affected him. He's pissed, though damn good at hiding it. For someone so solidly built, I marvel at the fact that he was once a sickly boy who needed a heart transplant just to have a shot at survival.

Or so he says.

Were he anyone else, I'd use his past as a delicate attempt to start a conversation and pry what little information from him I could. It would be so easy were we still in Terra Rodea, and I had the cloak of my father's power to hide behind. Why wouldn't it be? I've been bred to manipulate men and women alike, all with a coy grin.

This iteration of Domino Valenciaga makes me rethink my entire approach toward people—and my life as a whole. From day one, none of my attempts at friendliness—or otherwise—ever worked on him. Maybe I never was as charming or as pretty, or as sexy as I thought?

Or at least, not until he ensconced me in his private estate in the middle of only God knows where. Here, away from the city where I always believed I had influence, I could finally get him to fuck me.

And I hate myself for being proud of breaking down his barriers in such an insignificant way.

"Why don't you let me go now?" The question springs from my lips before I can rethink the pros and cons of asking it. "After all, if my father is dead—" I choke, barely able to spit out that word. "Then I'm of no danger to you. You have no worry of anyone seeking revenge."

"If?" He scoffs at the phrasing, his head lowered, hair hanging damply. "Don't be flattered by your presence here, Ada-Maria. I'll still give what's left of you to Jaguar when I'm done."

It's a horrifying threat that robs the air from my lungs, just as he intended it to.

And…

It's a lie. I'm not sure at first. Not until I parse over that subtle dip in his inflection. No, I don't think he intends for me to go to Jaguar.

Not anytime soon, at least.

And the confusion sowed by that thought is more than enough to dispel any exhaustion I may have felt. I sit forward, newly electrified with a desire to get a rise out of him. It seems to be the only way we communicate effectively.

Via taunts.

"You had no problem letting Alexi go to him," I point out, cringing at the feel of her name in my mouth. I hate the thought that he had his cock in her first. That he enjoyed her first.

That he did so without the excuse of hateful lust and that she had the nerve to smile after. She smiled like his attention was comparable to heaven itself—that elated fucking smirk porn stars spend years trying to emulate.

God, I hate her.

I hate him more. Enough that I don't take the tensing of his entire body as a warning sign like I should.

"Is that what this is about?" I continue stupidly. "Revenge? He stole your woman, and so you have penis envy—"

"*Finally.*" Pulling away from the wall, he whirls on me. "That mouth says something relevant for fucking once. Say it again."

Penis, I presume, because he grabs his, cupping his fingers along the engorged shaft. I feel my eyes bulge. How could I miss the extent of his erection until now?

Does the topic of Jaguar fucking his women get him so horny?

No, I realize as he stalks in my direction, spraying droplets of water as he goes. It's anger that arouses him. Rage. Disgust. All things inspired by *me* alone.

When he's close enough, he cups my chin, tilting it. I grit my teeth experimentally, wondering if I have the strength to resist the intention written in his gaze.

I don't. He merely flexes his fingers, and my lips fly apart.

"These lips," he murmurs, shocking me further by stroking the underside of my jaw with his thumb. "Some men would kill to have a mouth like this at their disposal."

Still holding me, he returns his opposite hand to his cock. In this position, I'd only have to lean forward to have access to him—and the way he tilts his hips in a silent demand makes it clear that's exactly what he wants. Me at his beck and call like a worthless whore. Like trash, as disposable as he claimed I am. My cheeks heat with shame.

Though why should I feel that way?

I'm not the man absently praising a woman he hates. He assumes there's power in degrading me. But I am a Pavalos.

We were born into power and taught from day one how to claim it. The catch is that I never had to do so without my father's commands, but there is no better time than now to start.

Meeting his gaze, I hold it, leaning forward of my own accord to graze the tip of him with my tongue. He lurches, and I savor the brief moment of triumph. He claims to own me, but he can't own *this*.

If I ignore the man, his cock is a beautiful specimen. He's circumcised, his arousal so thick already, he's practically pulsating. Were I the whore he claimed I am, his beauty alone would make his personality easy to overlook.

Warily, I cup him in the palm of my hand, testing the formidable weight. Aided by the warmth of the water, he's molten, and I feel a jolt shoot through my core.

"You look at my cock like it's a lollipop." His cool remark complicates my desire to ignore him. To thwart me further, he grips my chin, forcing me to meet his amused stare.

"Let's see what that beautiful little mouth can do. Open it."

I bristle at the command. *No.* This moment feels as fragile as he proved my body can be against his violence. If I let him dominate me in this arena, I might as well roll over and present my throat for the killing blow.

This brief power, and my sexuality…

They're all I have, and I own both by delivering a slow, savoring lick to the underside of his shaft despite his warning.

His shock is a thing of twisted beauty. He groans, his head shooting back while the hand on my chin slides down to my throat, almost in a grateful caress. Then he squeezes so tightly my eyes bulge.

"I told you to open," he grates.

Choking down any doubt, I lick him again, going slower, so slow the entire world seems to come to a screeching halt, hinging on the time it takes my tongue to clear the length of his shaft.

"*Dios mío…*" His voice is constricted with a grudging hint of something that could be pleasure, paired with his low grunt of annoyance. The hand around my throat sinks into my hair, cinching a fistful. "I told you to—"

I cup him again, curling my fingers around his impressive width. Then I stroke, up and down, each time with increasing amounts of pressure.

He breathes out roughly, his head still tilted back, eyes on the ceiling above. The shower spray continues to pelt us in that faint, fine mist, but the sensation acts like a cloud, obscuring us from the rest of the world.

In here, only the two of us exist, battling for control of this secluded realm. I aim to win. I have to—there isn't any other choice.

"Damn you." His anger is palpable in the vibrations running through me as he speaks. "Obey me. Open your fucking mouth—"

"I want you to make me come, instead," I gasp out, the first request that pops into my head. My aim is merely to test how far I can push him—nothing else.

And his soft, startled grunt shouldn't make my stomach flip. His brows shoot together, eyes like slits, and I nearly back down. Almost. But I'm genuinely curious of the answer to a question only he has ever made me bold enough to ask.

"Can you? Just with your cock, nothing else?" It's a fantasy I used to mull over in agony while in my old bed, forced to make do with my own fingers, while the Domino I thought I knew ignored me.

Here and now, the real man doesn't even try to disguise his interest. His expression shifts as he processes the challenge. When he grazes my windpipe with the tips of his fingers, I expect him to grip it, forcing my mouth open. Instead, he withdraws…

Only to snatch a length of my hair in the same breath. Viciously, he tugs, yanking me to my feet, wrenching me around so that my back is to him, my hands forced to brace against the wall of the stall.

He gives me no forewarning. No preparation. Only the water basting our bodies provides him any lubrication as he slams inside of me with a ferocity so intense, I cry out—that and the fact that I'm already wet for him. He hisses as my readiness drags him deep—so deep that his balls smack against my inner thighs, driving home the depth he's reached.

It should hurt, I think.

But it doesn't.

It stings, and it burns, and it's terrifying just how *good* it feels.

I should hate this man, vomit at his mere touch.

And yet, he has me moaning in a way I never have. Only as he abruptly withdraws do I realize he imparted that single thrust. Nothing more.

"You think you can command me," he murmurs against my throat. Then he bites, raking his teeth down to my shoulder. My startled cry nearly drowns out his next words. "I am the one in control here, Ada—" He jerks me around to face him, his eyes glowing, teeth bared. "Do you understand that?"

"Yes," I croak. But, before I can talk myself out of it, I run my hands down his chest, hoping to further distract him. I've already found the ridge of his surgical scar by the time he angles his gaze toward my rebellious fingers, his brows furrowing. "But I was just curious," I murmur, letting my voice meld with the hum of the shower spray.

He inclines his head, betraying the fact that he's listening to me at all. Yet, he has enough pride not to ask me the question my coy answer demands.

So, I give it to him anyway. "I was curious," I say, arching against his chest. This close, I can feel his breath catch, his muscles going rigid. Especially when I bring my mouth near his ear. "I wanted to know how quickly I could come on your cock. How good it could be… So that when you sell me, I can be confident I'll please my buyer—"

Snarling, he snatches my throat, bucking his hips at the same time. Fire. I'm suffocating and stuffed…and it's…

Incredible. A cry builds and sticks in my lungs as he tightens his grip, shoving me down onto the bench. He releases me, only to snatch my legs, one in each hand, and hike them against his hips as he pistons.

The harsh surface beneath me bites into my lower back like a brutal anchor as my thoughts become less coherent with every punishing thrust.

I've never been used like this. *Ridden* is the only term I can think of to describe it. Taken.

And thoroughly enjoyed by the bastard doing so.

Grunting, Domino throws his head back, his throat cording, nails piercing my flesh with every stroke. He couldn't hide his pleasure if he tried, and the more I watch him, the easier it is to forget. And hate.

And ignore how long I craved to have him inside me just like this.

Soon, it's too dizzying to look at him. I just close my eyes, surrendering to the pleasure ripping through my body, piece by piece. My impending orgasm is a death sentence and looms closer with every harsh stroke of his cock. Each brutal shove as he draws me into him.

But it isn't until I hear his voice, hoarse and grated, "Fuck… Ada—" that I finally feel it hit with the force of a crushing blow.

I hate that it feels as good as it does.

I hate that he's proved my little dare to be a reality—he can make me come like this, with only his cock, deployed as a weapon however he sees fit.

I'm still writhing when I feel him pull out, shoving me away. Boneless, I slump off the bench, landing on my knees against the damp floor as the water continues to pelt us both.

I hear him move, and I look up to find him snatch a rag from a built-in shelf and briskly wash himself off. Then he throws it aside and steps from the stall, storming into the bathroom, presumably to get a towel.

I don't know how much time passes before his voice finally reaches back to me. "We're done. Get out."

The water shuts off a heartbeat later, leaving me drenched, but still unclean. His seed mingles with the droplets of moisture dripping down my inner thighs.

A fact he is well aware of, I realize, as I look up to find him barring the entrance, a cream-colored towel slung around his waist. He doesn't offer me one of my own. Instead, he jerks his chin. "I said get out."

Rather than argue, I stand, surprised to find myself limping after him. I must have struck my hip when I fell, but I welcome the pain. Every fiery, throbbing jolt grounds me, reaching past the drunken haze of sex to reinforce the grim reality lurking beneath.

He's a bastard who sold me and killed my parents.

What the hell am I doing here?

I go still mid-step, pondering just that. I'm so lost in the daze that I miss the second he comes for me until it's too late. He already has a grip on my forearm, forcefully steering me back against the row of granite countertops.

Without a word of explanation, he snatches my hips, lifting me unceremoniously so that I'm sitting on the hard surface —with him standing in between my legs. I instinctively try to close them, but he doesn't budge, fixated on my left thigh. Already, a deep red mark is visible, stretching from my hip to my knee. I can tell merely from how it aches that it will bruise.

"At least I've proven I can ignore pain," I croak, hating how conditioned I sound already. Broken. "That will please my buyer, too. You might get a better price—"

He hisses through his teeth, silencing me mid-taunt. I just watch him instead, riveted by the slow, careful way he drags his finger along the mark, pressing down so hard I wince. It's as if he's remembering every mottled bit of flesh, noting how easily I bruise.

Not to denote on some fucked-up seller's manifest.

But so *he* can do it all over again.

And again, and again.

"Get dressed." He pulls away without remarking on the pile of clothing I've already selected for myself. I'm sure he can tell from the shape and color who they belong to.

He must be too distracted by his own thoughts to engage in another battle of wills so soon. Or, he's preoccupied with another matter entirely. His hand lands on the counter just beyond my reach, snatching up a familiar brown object as I flinch—his watch. Coiling his fingers over it, he cocks his head toward me. "By the way, Ada-Maria," he adds, his voice ragged. "At *La Guarida del Tigre,* they won't care how much pain you can endure. They'll only want to hear how loudly you can scream. I suggest you think about that as you process how little time you have left." Still sporting his towel, he strolls onto the balcony and disappears from view.

I collapse, landing hard on my knees, tasting blood as I bite my lower lip to smother the scream still building in my throat. I almost succeed, reducing the noise to just a pathetic gasp that echoes for a split-second before I scramble to my feet, drowning it out.

I eye my carefully selected outfit and consider just leaving this room naked. I feel trapped again. Like even if the thought felt like my own, wearing his shirt would only cement this strange hold he thinks he has over me. Ownership. The ability to decide whether I live or die.

And how.

But as my gaze flits to the doorway again, I realize that the second option is far less appealing, knowing that Alexi Rojas is lurking somewhere beyond this room as well, ready and waiting to gloat.

I snatch the shirt and pull it on, then scramble into the boxers. By the time I cross the balcony and re-enter his room, Domino is already dressed, buttoning a crisp black shirt all the way up to his neck.

I watch him, hating the glimmer of appreciation that hits my chest before I can help it. He can seem so graceful when he wants to.

And so cruel when he needs to.

He rakes his gaze over me before strolling into the hallway. Automatically, I start to follow, and I've barely reached the threshold when I find the door slammed in my face.

A harsh click warns that he locked it, though I test the doorknob anyway. It won't budge.

"Domino!" I slam my hand against the wooden surface, but the only response I hear is the sound of his steps retreating down the hall, away from me.

The bastard locked me in, but for whatever reason—in the grand scheme of everything he's done within the past twenty-four hours alone—this unnerves me the most. It heralds a different mode of operation apart from his usual indifference when it comes to my captivity.

This is possessive. Or selfish. Is he keeping me from Alexi on purpose, afraid of what she might say? Or of what I could learn…

Though, the most likely explanation is that he's gone to fuck her uninterrupted.

Of all the people in the world to trigger the crippling jealousy biting through my chest, it has to be them. A childhood enemy and a longtime hidden threat, both who hate my family and me for their own reasons.

The devil himself couldn't have picked a better pair. They belong together. I hope he fucks her raw in the shower and they both trip, earning lethal concussions that will make my escape a literal walk in the park.

I try not to imagine it—but it's too late; I already am. His body hunched over hers, that sly, stupid smile on her lips, her perky tits bouncing.

He wouldn't bite her, I bet.

He wouldn't fuck her hard enough to bruise.

He wouldn't swear one minute that she was his and sell her to a stranger the next.

The only man who should be on my mind is Jaguar, my supposed buyer—or at least the owner of the place Domino sold me to, *La Guarida del Tigre*. Despite my limited knowledge of the Spanish language, I can hazard a guess as to the meaning—The Tiger's den.

"The world is a zoo," my father told me once, his voice roughened by his nighttime cigar. It was the hour before he usually retreated to bed, when he'd exchanged his suit for a robe and slippers. That wasn't the most jarring change, though—that time of night was one of the rare few when his trusty Domino wasn't by his side, already having retired for the evening.

The lack of his "shadow" humbled him somehow. He could have been a normal man—if you ignored the gleam in his eye that warned he was always scheming, no matter who was in his orbit.

The world is a zoo, Ada-Maria. You can either be a warden or a beast. Do you understand that? He reached out, grazing my chin with the tips of his fingers. *Without me, all those bastards would be salivating to eat you alive. No matter what happens with this fucking indictment, you remember this—you are a Pavalos. Without me, you are nothing but a morsel they can't wait to devour. Together, we will always hang on to the keys to this kingdom. Loyalty, that's what matters. You fucking remember that...*

His voice fades beneath the squawk of a nearby bird, and I shiver despite the stifling heat.

If that memory serves a purpose, it's to remind me that Domino is no longer my main obstacle. In fact, I should ignore him entirely.

The world is a zoo, and I need to fend for myself, damn him and the cage he's designed around me. Shedding his shirt, I give in to the petty rage and step onto the balcony naked. The sun is just starting to rise, though hidden behind a swath of gray clouds. This section of the estate feels more secluded than the sprawling terrace. I can only see the tail end of the structure from here, as well as the shadow of two people strolling across the second level of it.

Alexi. I'd recognize her slender frame anywhere, her clothing so skimpy it just resembles lines of color across her torso and hips. She's standing beside someone taller, their bulky frame etched onto my psyche.

Domino.

He locked me in here just in time for a morning stroll. I don't know what feels worse—knowing that I'm just a hole to him? Or realizing that he doesn't even think highly enough of me to throw the fact that we've fucked in Alexi's face.

He's hiding me here out of shame.

How sweet.

The rush of anger blinds me to everything else—like the fact that another figure is standing within view of me, though from a different part of the property. On the far right, a section of circular, flat stone is visible—near the front of the house, I realize, though positioned diagonally from the terrace as a whole. Set within a section of hedges and tended flower beds, I assume it's a driveway, given the set of black cars parked there. Beside one, holding the driver's side door partially open, stands a man whose shape makes me go rigid. Him, I don't recognize as easily as Domino.

Not until I hear his voice.

He whistles, his laughter booming enough to echo across the property. "Well, good fucking morning," he calls to me.

My cheeks sear as I realize that he can see me—and my lack of clothing—clearly. Automatically, I raise my hands, attempting to shield myself.

Then I stop, my fingers raised just beneath my nipples.

From the corner of my eye, I see the distant shape of Domino go rigid, like a speck of darkness over the otherwise bright landscape. I know he's watching me. I can practically feel his eyes raking over my skin with that unspoken possession.

Don't. I can almost hear him voicing the warning in his signature unstable rasp. *Don't you fucking dare.*

I don't take my eyes off him, even as I lift my hand and wave toward the figure in the driveway. He chuckles, whistling even louder. Something in the sound sends a shiver of unease through me. It's primal, like the way one of my father's dogs would snarl when it had a bone it didn't want to share with the others.

A warning.

When I look back at Domino, however, he's gone. It's like he vanished, leaving Alexi standing alone.

At least until I hear a door open and slam with the force of a gunshot.

CHAPTER THREE

"What the hell are you doing?" His voice is softer than it should be, perfectly controlled to not be overheard by anyone beyond this room. "Come here—"

"Why?" I'm still watching Jaguar and his posse. They look dangerous, even from afar. The sort of men my father would meet miles from the city when he thought no one saw him. A reporter did once and threatened to blackmail him, using photographic evidence.

Until my father sent me to charm my way into his office and plant materials that he reported stolen from our house earlier that week, ensuring the man was jailed and unable to access his so-called evidence. At least until he was released on bail and found all of his electronics smashed to pieces. Such was the way my father handled any threat.

With vicious, underhanded tactics or outright bribery.

Whatever he wanted protected, he hid under lock and key, deploying them only when necessary. Whether he realizes it or not, Domino's been acting the same way—obscuring his hatred toward my family, then revealing Pia's diary…

And by taking me now?

Trying to decipher his motives hurts my brain. Banishing all thoughts of him, I relish the heat of the weakened sun on my body, counting down the seconds that pass without him dragging me inside.

Then, some harrowing moment between Jaguar's next whistle and my own heartbeat, I realize that he won't. He *can't*.

Because to do so would risk breaking his façade before the one person he seems determined to hide me from. Alexi or Jaguar?

That's the real question.

When I turn to face him, I can't glean an answer from his expression alone. All I find is pure, molten rage.

His teeth flash, the only break in the shadows that shroud most of his expression. "Get in."

I don't refuse him outright. I just brace my elbows against the balcony on either side of me and lean back, feeling my heart race like mad. I'm terrified. I'm also resigned.

Honestly, in this moment, I feel like I wouldn't have any problem at all with leaning back further. Too far. Falling over this balcony entirely and landing on the rugged terrain below.

He must realize that, but the prospect alarms him enough to stalk forward, coming into view of our audience below. I watch his eyes, waiting to see who they flicker toward first.

Unsettlingly, they remain fixated on me, a writhing mass of brown and flecks of green, promising a wrath unlike any I've experienced from him so far.

For a second, I rock on my heels, testing how much force it would truly require to actually hurl myself over the edge.

Too late.

He reaches me within a fraction of a second, palming the side of my face to pull me close.

"You have no idea what game you're playing, Ada-Maria," he murmurs, his tone so level and soft it's damn near gentle. His hands betray his malice, however, shaking against my skin as if it's requiring every ounce of restraint he has just to keep from ripping me apart.

"I think I *do*," I counter, shocked by how hard my voice sounds in comparison to his.

His eyes narrow—he's shocked as well.

Possessed by whatever boldness has taken hold of me, I keep talking. "I think I'm showing the man you sold me to what he can expect once he completes his purchase."

I wince at the intensity his eyes take on. Something beyond anger, beyond rage.

"Oh, how I will punish you for that," he growls, lowering his mouth against my ear. "You have no fucking idea of the danger you are in. The sheer *stupidity* of what you're doing—"

"Then tell me." I'm louder than he is, threatening to break the show he's putting on.

Touching me like this…

From the outside, I know what it will look like. Like I'm out here with his permission—that his relationship with me is cordial enough to permit him to stroke my cheek and stand so close.

But why? It's not the expected behavior a man would show toward a woman he's brutalized and kidnapped.

And relenting to his touch isn't the way one would expect such a woman to act toward her captor.

I must twitch or make some move to pull away because he's closer, using his body weight to practically crush me against the railing.

"Get the fuck inside." His tone loses any shred of control; it's rippling, verging on something too primal to be considered speech. "You dumb, stupid cunt. You have no idea what you've done. None!"

But said ignorance isn't any fault of my own. It strikes me now that, against his demands, I have one last card to play, however fragile it may be.

I raise my hand, cupping the back of his. As a result, his nails scrape against my cheek in a silent warning—but I'm playing along.

For now.

"Then tell me," I demand.

Finally, his eyes dart away from me, and I have my answer as to whose presence has him on edge—Jaguar's. Whatever he sees triggers a flicker of alarm across his expression.

The next thing I know, his mouth is on mine, his hands roughly cupping my hips, pulling me into him. From the outside, it must look like a sexy, heated kiss filled with lust and passion.

In reality, his teeth seize onto my lower lip, preventing any chance I could easily pull away. With his strength, he snatches me to him, maneuvering me from the balcony and within the room in seconds.

Once we're away from view, he shoves me so hard I go flying, barely managing to catch myself on the edge of the mattress.

"You will pay for this," he warns, his voice ice. "You—"

"Tell me why or I'll scream," I croak, still stunned by how quickly he moved.

The threat, however, must slip beneath his armor. He flinches, his eyes slits as I open my mouth and suck in air in preparation.

"Tell me—"

"You aren't supposed to know that I've sold you." He says it so tonelessly. As if he's referring to a pair of shoes and not a woman. Me. My body. My life.

Voice rasping, the only reply I can choke out is, "W-What?"

"Why *would* I tell you?" he adds, closing the door to the balcony with a thud. Arms crossed, he starts to pace, his back to me. Ironically, it's reminiscent of the times I would watch him in the dark, performing this very act in front of my family's guest house, seeming as though the weight of the world rested on his shoulders. "As far as Jaguar knows, you think I've rescued you from the attack that killed your boyfriend. You think you're safe under my protection here. It minimizes the risk to him for you to be in the dark."

He doesn't laugh or sneer. He's telling the truth.

In Jaguar's eyes, I'm his simpering little fool.

"You… You unimaginable bastard." My voice breaks. I almost can't fathom the cruelty—let alone the thought that he's telling the truth. That could have easily been my reality if I didn't regain consciousness to overhear his two goons discussing his ownership of me.

He even said it himself—*I aimed to use her ignorance to my advantage.*

The worst part that I find truly horrifying is that it could have worked. In a different world, I could have easily been lulled into a false sense of safety, believing he was my savior. In fact, that was my first hope soon after I awoke here.

And he took great pains to reveal that hope for what it was —fragile and pathetic.

"Why?" I demand. "Why tell me at all? Do you get off on my fear?"

Or maybe he truly hates me that much. He couldn't even endure a lie long enough to gain my trust and have me put my faith in him. I am *that* repulsive to him.

The thought stings, but he never takes the chance to drive the truth home, right when it will hurt me the most. When I look up, he's watching me, his expression devoid of any hint of emotion. He might as well be stone.

"You know what I want," he says.

And maybe I do.

"Pia," I rasp. Drawing my knees to my chest, I hunch over myself, suddenly aware of how naked I am in comparison to him. "You think she's dead, and you think I know where some file my father had is. Because you are her brother."

Navid.

Surprisingly, he doesn't deny it outright. He cocks his head as if weighing my word choice. Apparently, I got some details wrong.

"You *know* where she is," he says softly. "Maybe you think you don't, but somewhere in that vapid, fucking brain is the answer. I'm sure of that."

"You're wrong," I say. I don't think I've ever heard my voice sound so hollow. So hopeless.

Can I even blame him?

I could play the victim and ignore the things I've done to Pia. I may not have killed her, but I certainly betrayed her. I conspired against her, and I shunned her without hearing her side.

Though who could blame me?

She slept with my father and used me to get to him, just as Domino seems determined to use me. And my father…

That's all my life has been—being used, and used, and used.

"Where do you think you're going?" Domino demands.

I'm staggering to my feet, heading for the balcony despite him moving to stand in front of me.

"I'm going to see if Jaguar is still here and beg him to take me with him—"

"Don't!" He snatches my arm, yanking me back. "You have no fucking idea who he is. You think he'll be your knight in shining armor? You are dead wrong, Ada-Maria."

"I don't care."

And I don't.

"Wait—" He tightens his grip when I attempt to take another step.

"Why should I?" I pull back to see his face, but I'm not prepared for the expression I find. Not one of hate. Instead, his eyes are narrowed, his head tilted as though he's contemplating a puzzle he only has seconds to solve.

"I want to find Pia's body," he admits, pulling me even closer.

Not because he truly thinks I can break away, but because he's that worried about being overheard. Whatever he's saying, he does so while being fully cautious of Jaguar, despite the other man being yards away outside of the house.

"Help me, and you will have my protection. Trust me, it's a better offer than anything else you'll be presented with."

"I…" *Don't know* is my first impulsive reply. Truly I don't. If Pia is dead, she could be anywhere. Besides, Domino has worked with my father; if anyone would have an idea of where he'd bury the body of a dead girl over a decade ago, it would be him.

And yet, something makes me swallow those words before I can fully voice them.

He means what he said to me—*you will have my protection.* It could be a lie, or another mind game. In the grand scheme, he could just sell me to Jaguar once he's through with me and never look back.

But he's right.

I don't have a better option.

Why not get some leverage over him, no matter how fragile, and bide my time until a better opportunity comes along?

"Jaguar is a dangerous man, Ada-Maria," he warns, still speaking in an undertone, his jaw practically pressed against mine. "You have no idea what he's capable of, the things he will do to you if he gets the chance. I am your only hope of surviving with that pretty little body intact."

"Fine." It pains me to choke down a nasty retort and face him while keeping my expression blank.

He's wary, his eyes slits as they scan my gaze, hunting for any sign of deceit. I don't know if I aim to reassure him, or I merely have to hear myself say it out loud to believe it.

"I'll play your game if you promise to protect me. I'll do what I can to help you find Pia."

That phrasing makes it not an outright lie.

But he didn't miss it. "You lead me to Pia's body if you want a damn thing from me," he warns. "In the meantime, you prance around here like a happy little cum whore, and you let Jaguar and his spy believe that you are oblivious to everything. I am your hero who rescued you from a living nightmare after you watched your boyfriend be murdered right in front of you. Understand?"

I don't. My head is spinning, trying to juggle it all, and now I know why he locked me in here—to protect his lie.

And yet, it betrays a rare hint of vulnerability on his part that he's even revealed as much to me.

"I guess this means that you have no need to lock your naïve, captive bunny rabbit in a bedroom without her consent, then," I croak. His nostrils flare, his grip on my arm tightening—but the display alone reveals that I'm right. Therefore, I don't mind twisting the knife just a little more. "I guess that means no more collar, either."

"Don't forget that Jaguar knows I injured you badly enough to require an extra week for you to heal, Ada-Maria. This isn't some fairy tale fucking romance—"

"How *did* you explain it?" I ask, jutting my chin as I parse through what few possible explanations I can come up with. None make sense. "Why would any woman stay with you willingly after what you've done? Why would my 'hero' collar me and have me whipped?"

"Do you really want to know?" He smiles, but it's a grotesque distortion of his mouth, nothing more. "I told him you like it rough—" He releases me, retreating toward another corner of the room. A second later, a wad of fabric lands against my chest, thrown by him. "Get dressed. And if you want to extend your life beyond Tuesday, you'll do what I say—which is keep your mouth shut."

The clothing he gave me is his, I realize. His shirt, which I pull on without complaint, too distracted by his revelation to care that, in this context, my little stunt has lost all its meaning.

No longer am I toying with his boundaries, but playing right into his sick narrative. His loyal, love-struck captive would, of course, choose to wear an item of his.

Did Alexi?

Her presence here irritates me more the longer I ponder Domino's reaction to her. He kept pictures of him fondling her naked body in his closet. And yet, how did he refer to her?

Jaguar's spy…

"Ines will bring you your lunch here," Domino says.

I look over my shoulder to find him entering the hall. From the way he reaches for the doorknob, I can tell what he intends to do.

Lock me in.

"I thought you said I could leave?"

He scoffs. "I am not as dumb as I look, Ada-Maria, and you are not as convincing as you think you are. I've humored you this once, but if you want my trust, batting your eyelashes and showing off your tits isn't how you get it. You *earn* it. Or so help me God, I will get that collar you like so much, wrap it around your throat and tie you in the closet like an animal for the week. Jaguar be damned. Do you understand that?"

He doesn't give me the chance to answer.

He slams the door, and a definitive click that sounds after reveals that he wasn't bluffing.

I'm locked in.

Quickly, though, I realize that I'm not completely without a weapon of my own.

I almost miss it as I pace, tearing my fingers through my hair as I consider going back onto that balcony and screaming bloody murder for anyone to hear.

He left it on the glass case of watches in the middle of the closet, perhaps as his own twisted attempt at a peace offering.

Or a taunt.

The pink surface mocks me as I approach it and warily run my fingers across the cover. Apart from last night, I haven't touched this object in ten years. A decade.

Plenty of time for Pia's lies and schemes to come back to bite me.

You think you're so different from me? she screamed at me during one of the last times I ever saw her. *You're just a selfish, spoiled little bitch who can't see beyond her stupid life. The rest of us? We're not so lucky, Ada. I don't have a papa to snap his fingers and fix my problems!*

I'd been so angry; I could have exploded. Never, had I felt that kind of rage before, or since. *So that's why you had to fuck him, then?* I'd thrown back at her. *Who's the bitch now?*

She blinked, her green eyes blazing, glistening with unshed tears. I'll never forget the look she gave me. Almost one of pity. *You have no idea what the hell is going on, do you? God, you're pathetic, Ada. Just give me my fucking diary back, and we can forget this ever happened…*

But it was too late by then, of course.

I'd already given it to my father.

And I'd already read every word.

CHAPTER FOUR

This time, I don't read a single page of the diary.

Maybe I'm just not brave enough. Or the avoidance is more an act of defiance than anything else. As much as he pretends not to, Domino badly wants me to help him decipher whatever mysteries his sister left behind. He's desperate enough to hope that the answer to her supposed death lurks within those pages.

Though why should I help him? My own self-interest aside, trusting him would be foolish. If my father did kill Pia, and I lead him to her body, only God knows what he'd do to me in retaliation.

He's already claimed to have killed my parents as well as Tristan.

Using the past as a predictor of the future, he'll more than likely shoot me himself and bury me in Pia's grave.

If there even *is* a grave.

A part of me still can't buy it—which makes the revelation that Domino might be her brother even harder to stomach. He would know, wouldn't he? If his sister were alive. She would have tried to contact him at least once within the past ten years?

Or Pia turned out to be the same old Pia, as selfish and cruel as I remember.

Though, even as a part of me desperately wants to cling to that belief, I can't. Pia may have hated me, but she loved her brother. His name dominated the pages of that diary, from what I can recall. Her entire justification for stealing the amount of money she did was for him.

His surgery.

I have to wonder if, indirectly, Roy Pavalos paid for the transplant he inevitably received. That would make his betrayal far, far worse, I decide. To betray the man whose fortune saved your life, no matter his supposed crimes.

Only a monster would do that.

Though, to be fair, Domino doesn't seem to have any idea as to who his sister truly was. Can I blame him? For the longest time, she had me fooled as well.

I loved her like a sister.

But to her, I was nothing but an obstacle to overcome.

The painful thought spurs me as far away from the diary as possible. Thankfully, he didn't lock the door to the balcony. As I escape into the warm, mid-morning air, I find that

Jaguar—and his posse—is gone. So is Alexi from her position on the terrace. An image of her and Domino fucking somewhere else, in some distant room of the house, sneaks into my skull, and I don't have the strength to block it out.

I hate that I can't predict him. Despite five years of knowledge regarding the man he used to be, I'm forced to admit that I know nothing about who he is.

Apart from what turns him on, of course. I know that a smart mouth—literally and figuratively—gets him going. But nowhere near as much as the sight of blood can.

My blood.

Here, in the warm, humid air far from prying eyes, there's nothing to stop me from reliving those sordid moments. Over and over again.

His touch. His pleasured moans rippling through my eardrum. His breath, hot on my throat. His taste.

His chest.

I keep seeing the stark, surgical line that denotes a past I can't deny. Whether or not he truly is Navid Inglecias, he's suffered. Suffering that he seems to blame my father for— and, indirectly, me. It certainly puts an ironic twist on my past attraction to him, anyway.

To crave a man without a heart… His own, at least. It's why his body can fuck me despite the hatred he harbors inside.

And yet, he's the only man to truly make me feel…anything remotely close to pleasure during sex.

How goddamn sad is that?

Ines comes hours later, leaving a tray of food for me on the bed.

I ignore it, barely paying it a glance on my way into the bathroom. I strip his shirt, leaving it carelessly over the threshold, and approach the now empty shower stall.

It's an exercise in clicking through various options on the digital control panel before I manage to get the water running. Safe within this glass cocoon, I lean against the granite wall and force myself to think.

If my father did kill Pia all those years ago, where could she be?

In our backyard? It's an obvious guess, but one I can easily rule out—my mother would have long since found her during all of the many renovations she's had done to the property in the last decade. I'm sure during the tennis court reno, it might have gotten back to us if the workers stumbled upon the body of a fifteen-year-old girl.

It isn't long, however, before my thoughts turn away from Pia to the man who claims to be her long-lost older brother.

Because he's here.

His scent packs a physical punch despite the overall stealth of his entrance. He watches me for a while, from beyond this realm of glass. I can see him from the corner of my eye, a shadow over the gray color scheme.

Eventually, he grows bored of merely watching. Without bothering to disguise his entrance, he slides open the glass door—slowly enough for the cool air to battle with the wall of steam I've let build up.

I don't turn to see if he's naked or not. When I sense him claim the bench across from me, I move to a different corner of the stall, finding a hook where he left the washcloth from this morning.

He never let me clean myself, I realize. Even now, I can feel the remnants of him, stubbornly clinging to my innermost, sensitive parts. Snatching the rag, I find a bar of scented soap and work it into a lather. Then I take my time, scrubbing every last inch of my body.

I'm methodical, so intent on my work that I almost forget he's watching.

"You think you can ignore me?" he asks, his voice heavy, though I don't detect his usual anger.

A good fucking session could do that to a man, leaving him languid and relaxed after.

Enough! I shake my head to clear it and run the rag between my breasts, then over my stomach—all without paying him a single glance.

"I like you quiet, Ada-Maria," he continues, still sounding as if he's across the stall. He hasn't moved.

Yet.

"I don't think I like you bitter, though. Your lips aren't meant to be pursed so tightly. The expression ages you."

I scoff, giving him the attention he wants. "Don't tell me you're partial to my father's tastes. How did you put it? Young, dumb, blond—"

"I'm not talking about any other woman, am I?" he counters in a tone that makes me grip my washcloth tighter. "I'm talking about you."

"Me," I echo hoarsely. "The woman you hate. The woman you hurt and have brutalized. The woman who hates you."

"You couldn't fuck a man you hated the way you fuck me."

I feel my mouth fall open at his bluntness. The worst part? He sounds confident—too confident.

As if he's studied how I fuck in general, well enough to make an educated inference.

"I'm good at faking it, Domino," I counter. Finally, I gather the nerve to meet his gaze from over my shoulder.

There is no sly, mocking smile on his face. He's dead serious.

"That you are," he agrees, seated on the bench, leaning back against the wall. He's naked, I realize, my cheeks flaming. The water pelts him, glistening off his skin and erasing any traces of sweat or exertion that he might have sported beforehand. "You are a damn good faker, at least for a man who doesn't know any fucking better."

I shiver, turning away to face the wall as I continue to wash myself. "You seem sure of that."

"Because I am," he replies. "Your boyfriend videotaped nearly every time he fucked in that penthouse of his—you, along with the many other women he was toying with. If it makes you feel any better, you were by far the sexiest. The bastard came faster with you than any other."

I stiffen, horrified by how callously he can reveal such intimate acts. Is he telling the truth? Only God knows. Tristan, the bastard, wasn't known for his faithful nature. I'd suspected his affair with Alexi early on, but am I surprised if she wasn't the only one?

But therein lies another secret revealed by Domino's admission—*you were by far the sexiest.* Is he including Alexi in that assessment?

God, I shouldn't care…

"The second I heard you moan for real, I realized how damn good of an actress you are," he continues, his voice loud and booming. Gone is the gruff undertone he took on with Jaguar in earshot. He's shameless now, uncaring of who might overhear.

Perhaps, because he tired out Alexi well enough to know she's dead to the world.

"I am a good actress," I agree, dropping the washcloth. "So good I made you think you actually got me off, Domino—"

"Your fake moans are pretty," he continues as if I never spoke. "The real ones? Goddamn, Ada-Maria. You could drive a man insane with those cries. Whether you're in pain or in pleasure, it's the same damn tune."

My next breath sticks in my chest as my heart hammers like mad. Is he joking? I can't tell, and this time I'm not inclined to look for myself.

"Enjoy your shower." I start for the door, scrambling to slide it open.

"Tristan," he practically snarls the name, "never went down on you—at least not in any of the recordings. He never spread those legs and tasted that pussy for himself. I used to imagine how you'd taste."

The intensity of his voice takes my breath away. I hate that he almost sounds genuine, like he truly did just that—dwell on the taste of me.

"How did Alexi taste?" I demand, turning to face him.

He raises an eyebrow. "How do you think she tasted? Like fucking roses. Why don't you ask her?"

I flinch, gritting my teeth, desperate to disguise just how deeply that taunt cuts. So deep it hurts, outshining my general aches and pains. I hate the thought of him lying with her. Kissing her.

Tasting her with the same tongue I used to fantasize about tasting me.

Spotting my rag on the floor, I cross over to it, leaving the shower door partially ajar. Grabbing it, I turn to face him. "You want to know what I taste like, Domino?" My voice is a low, husky purr.

But I'm struck dumb by his reaction. He sits forward, his head cocked, eyes obscured by strands of black hair plastered to his forehead by the shower spray. They slice his face into slivers, each one more unreadable than the last.

His eyes track every step I take toward him, blazing and burning.

"Here—" I throw the rag at him so hard it rebounds off his chest and lands at his feet. "That's the only taste of me you'll ever get. Savor it."

My words ring hollow, of course. He's too strong to overpower on my own—and there's nothing stopping him from lurching to his feet and pinning me down, taking from me whatever he damn well pleases.

To my shock, he grabs the rag and brings it to his mouth. Slowly, he extends his tongue, dragging it across a section of the rag in a way that makes my cheeks flame, my body heating. Licking his lips, he sits back again.

"Like milk and honey," he says raggedly.

And I sway. He's tasting the flavor of the soap I used. Not me. Getting ahold of myself, I once again stagger for the exit.

"That shitty camera of his never showed your back in detail," he says with a certainty that makes me stop short, my horror returning in full. "I couldn't see your scars from the footage. Tell me who hurt you."

"Why? So you can get pointers?" I toss back, eyeing the sliver of the bathroom lurking beyond this fragile pane of glass. Freedom. All I have to do is take the necessary few steps to reach it.

One…

"No," he says so coldly I'm frozen again. "So, I can kill them."

It's a strange boast to come from a man who hates me so. He whips me. Collars me. Lies to me.

Then confesses that he mused about what I taste like and vows to kill the man he thinks hurt me.

Though, it's an empty threat.

We both know who whipped me and what happened to him.

"Luckily for you, he's already dead, Domino," I rasp, taking another step. I'm close enough to grip the edge of the sliding glass door—and I do, for dear life, rattling it on the metal rail keeping it in place.

The sound of him rising to his feet is loud enough to overpower that delicate clinging noise. There's the thud of the rag hitting the ground a second time, followed by the patter of water dripping from his body, and his slow, heavy footsteps as he advances toward me.

All I can do is watch as he grips the door above where my hand is, easily wrenching it shut. I barely manage to pull my fingers out of the way.

"I want you to tell me why he did it," he demands, his breath fanning the space between my shoulder blades, though I don't dare turn around to see him there behind me. "And you will, Ada-Maria. You'll tell me every fucking detail. Why? I'll do what I know you've been dreaming about since the day I first met you in your father's office."

"Leave?" I croak hopefully.

He laughs. At the same time, he takes his hand from the door and uses it to grip my chin, whirling me around to face him. The glass rattles again as he pins me against the cool surface.

I have no choice but to see his face—to see the eyes ruthlessly raking over my body as if he truly does own it. Every inch, long before he had me brought here.

"I'll taste you," he declares, his voice rippling with lust. "And I'll have you wishing that I put a bullet in that bastard's brain sooner."

Tristan? Or my father?

He doesn't clarify, and I'm too unnerved to ask. I don't want to know the answer.

"I'd rather die," I hiss, "than feel any part of you on me *anywhere!*"

"You should be dead." He traces my jawline with the pad of his thumb, roughly as if he's trying to memorize every inch by feel alone. When he nears my ear, he leans in, bringing his mouth against the lobe. "If it weren't for me, you would be. That bullet was meant for *you.*"

CHAPTER FIVE

That bullet was meant for you…

I gasp, overwhelmed by the implications of that statement. Then I recoil, shoving at his chest with both hands.

"You're sick! Get the fuck away from me—"

"Think, Ada-Maria," he demands, not budging an inch. "Ask yourself who had everything to gain if his daughter, keeper of his secrets, happened to die a horrific death the night before his impending arraignment."

His tone is different. Too persistent. Too cold. Too…believable.

"No!" I wrench away and yank the door open enough to squeeze from the stall. Tripping over the threshold, I stumble, losing my balance so that I wind up on my knees, gripping the edge of a counter for balance. "You're lying. Playing with my head. You're lying!"

"I'm not." God, he sounds so calm. So gentle?

No. No. No. I slap my hands over my ears and hum.

But nothing short of screaming could drown him out. "You were always a liability to him, but I wasn't sure until I saw those scars. A man who would beat his own daughter like that? He didn't give a damn whether you lived or died. He was only ever out for himself."

"That sounds like *you*." I whirl on him, hauling myself to my feet, utilizing the counter for balance.

He's still technically inside the shower stall, watching me from beyond the gap in the glass partition.

"You were the one who only ever gave a damn about himself. After what you claimed to have done to my father, don't you dare bring him into this."

"So he did whip you."

I groan in exasperation, feeling as though my brain is being manipulated and twisted, all for his amusement. "No. You did—"

"I didn't hurt you," he claims, still in that aggravatingly level tone.

"Oh really?" I hiss out a vicious excuse for a laugh. "You could have fooled me!"

"I merely punished you," he adds, taking a step to bridge the gap between the shower and the main bathroom. Behind him, the water continues to fall, creating steam that billows around him like smoke. He looks like a literal demon waltzing out of hell, and my pulse surges to a painful, pulsating rhythm.

"If I wanted to hurt you, Ada… Trust me, there are a million ways I could do so." He takes another step, exiting the shower completely, dripping water onto the floor. "And believe me when I say I've considered them all."

"You want to know something funny?" I rasp.

Though it isn't funny in the slightest. It's pathetic, a painful reality stabbing at the back of my mind, threatening to reduce me to tears if I think on it long enough.

"I'm used to men not living up to their hype. Tristan was a dick, but he never disappointed me. I never expected better from him. Not good sex, not real commitment, not even loyalty. I'm sure you know better than anyone that I only gave him the time of day because the relationship benefited my father. In fact, most of the men I've dated and fucked were just that—peons my father wanted to control, so he used me."

It sounds horrifying when said out loud; I can admit that. Internally, I've always processed it differently than I figure anyone outside of the family would. My father used me— but he *trusted* me, too. He relied on me. He needed me.

We had a bond forged by blood and family, strong enough to outlast everything.

Always.

But if one man ever came close to earning a glimmer of that same amount of loyalty from me, it certainly wasn't Tristan Lucas or any of my other conquests.

"Every man I ever met or interacted with, I never had any high hopes for," I admit hoarsely, staring down at the floor. "Why? I was always mentally comparing them to someone else. Someone who always won out. Always. And who was that?" My voice thickens as the threat of tears burns my eyes. I start to blink, hoping to keep them at bay.

It's too late. They fall, but in this instance, I jut my chin to brandish them like war paint. I'm not ashamed of them. They, better than anything I could say, prove how sincerely I mean the words leaving my throat. He can't deny them.

"It was you. Always, it was *you*. No one could ever measure up to the fictional version of Domino Valenciaga I built up in my head."

Not even the real man, as it turns out.

"Do you realize how pathetic that makes you? Tristan never had a chance in hell of measuring up, but you? You can't even match the man I *thought* you were."

That gets a rise out of him. His eyes darken, his head dipping low, and my heart stutters fearfully. With three heavy strides, he advances on me before I can even regain my balance fully.

His hand captures my chin, weighing it against his palm as though he's considering how easy it would be to crush it. I feel his fingers twitch excitedly—God, he wants to.

"I would watch you," he tells me. "Over and over, I'd watch those fucking videos of you with him."

Tristan?

"And not only that dumb son of a bitch." He brings his other hand up to stroke the damp hair from my face, dragging me closer until I'm straining on tiptoe. "Most of the men you've ever fucked within the past five years, I caught a glimpse, Ada. Of you, riding their dicks in the back of a fancy sports car or in that private cabana your father owns at the country club. I've heard you moan; I've seen that perky little ass bounce. I came up with the impression that you were a dumb slut, so easy that a fancy gift and a glass of wine could get you wet."

He trails off, giving me plenty of time to picture the twisted ways he's tried to emulate that. With his "gift" of a whip, and the imported vintage, he claimed to know I love.

"I see now that I was wrong, Ada. You failed to live up to even that rather generous impression of you. I thought you were too stupid to know better. That you enjoyed the lifeless sex and cheap affection. Why else subject yourself to man after man, after man who only saw you as an object? But now I see the truth about you."

He cradles my jaw in both hands, lowering his mouth enough to baste my lips in the warmth of his breath.

"You were never stupid, Ada-Maria. You were calculating, doing whatever your papa told you to, without even taking your own pleasure into account. I worked for the man to get close to him. To learn how best to overpower the sick bastard. But you? What did you get out of being his daughter other than shitty sex and learning how to best fake an orgasm? Oh, and don't let me forget—being beaten and whipped—"

Thwack! The unmistakable smack of flesh on flesh leaves me stunned. All I can do is brace myself for the pain I should feel—and I do, throbbing like hell, but not on my face or any other part of my body within his reach.

My hand hurts. I eye the reddening, trembling fingers and realize that I'm the one who struck him.

"I'll let you have that one hit," he says, running his hand across his mouth. He eyes his fingers, and even from here, I can see the streak of red painting them. He's bleeding from his bottom lip. "You can savor this, Ada," he adds. "I gave you one more thing that he couldn't."

And what might that be?

I'm not brave enough to ask.

"Stay away from me." I lunge toward the balcony and into the bedroom, entering it on my own, free from any assault on his part. With my eyes on the door to the hall, I keep moving.

"You never asked me why."

I glance back to find Domino still standing in the doorway, his hands braced against the wall on either side as if he's physically stopping himself from lunging for me.

"Why I watched you," he clarifies. "Why I know the most intimate details of your little rendezvouses. You could assume it was because I sought to satisfy my own twisted obsession—" He laughs, proving the folly of that suspicion. Ice cold, he cuts his eyes up to mine, drilling in the fact that everything he's about to say is the brutal, honest truth. "Or I was only doing my job. What my boss commanded of me. You see, he never trusted you. No matter how many times you fucked for him. Lied for him. It was never enough. He never saw you as anything more than a tool. You meant nothing to him."

I don't let myself process the hatefulness in those words. I just run, wrenching open the door and entering the hallway without another word from him. He doesn't follow me, either. I'm allowed to tear through the house, unbothered by anyone.

For the first time, I take notice of my surroundings beyond the confines of Domino's room. It's later in the evening, with the sunset visible beyond the windows, painting everything in a bloody red glow. If I were to run out of the front door and take my chances in the desert, at least I could do so without running the risk of getting heatstroke. Already, the air feels cooler, aided by the fact that I'm still naked, dripping wet.

Rather than forge ahead with another escape attempt, I find myself padding down the hallway before the white room I've subconsciously come to think of as my own—but when I throw open the door, I realize just how foolish I've been.

Nothing in this house is mine. He's already taken great pains to prove that.

By giving this room to someone else, he's merely reinforcing my status as his captive.

"Domino?" The voice identifies the blond woman lying sprawled across the white bed, her ass up, legs kicking at the air. She's wearing a black dress that I can tell was taken from the closet, her cleavage spilling out onto the sheets beneath her. Before her is a plate of ripe strawberries that she's picking at with her fingers.

"Took you long enough." She rolls over, her coy smile falling flat the second she sees me.

And I know instantly that I interrupted something. She was waiting for him.

"G-Get the fuck out," I rasp. It's all I can say. The thought of retreading my steps is too painful to bear. I can't leave this room. So I stumble across it, aiming for the only sanctuary I can spy at the moment—the closet.

"You look like you've been having fun," Alexi taunts, her tone just as bitchy as I remember. I can tell without having to look that she hasn't budged. She won't.

Not unless I give her a good enough reason to get her perky ass in motion.

"He's all warmed up for you," I tell her as I feel alongside the mirror for the latch to activate the door beneath. I can't even look at my reflection. I just close my eyes to everything, this room, this reality.

Even without the aid of drugs, I'm determined to float away. Refuse to exist in this space anymore.

"What the hell is your problem?" I hear Alexi snipe, her presence clashing with my attempts to fade. Zone out. Become numb.

The two of us were never as close to each other as we both were to Pia. She was the glue holding our impromptu group together, but looking back, I can't deny that I had fun moments with Alexi, too. She was the silly girl, always cracking jokes—the balancing force between Pia's aloof confidence and my shyness.

In her own way, she was a decent enough friend. She taught me how to wear lipstick, and tried to teach me how to flirt.

And, after Pia disappeared, she taught me what true loneliness could feel like.

"Are you just going to stand there?" Her voice startles me back to the present, as icy as ever.

"I told you I got his cock hard enough," I snap. "So why don't you do what you do best and go fuck my leftovers."

I don't wait to see if she heeds the offer this time. I peel my eyes open long enough to lunge inside the closet and slam the door behind me. Then I make my way into the furthest corner I can and curl into a ball small enough to wedge my body in between two shelves.

It's not my preferred hideout beneath the blankets, but it's close enough. Here, the world fades to a dull hum, only discernable if I choose to listen closely enough.

First, there's only silence. Endless, oppressive silence…

Then sobbing. Such loud, wracking, frantic cries as though the person voicing them is on the verge of utterly breaking apart. They can't be coming from me.

I've been through enough hurt and rejection by now that nothing should be able to break me down. No one should be able to reduce me to a sniveling, sobbing mess.

Especially if they've only voiced the truth I already know.

My father never loved me.

He needed me.

But in my world, those are the same damn thing.

CHAPTER SIX

"Have you ever been in love?" Pia asked me once. The question came from nowhere, uttered in her typical crisp, confident tone. But I could sense something lurking beneath her seemingly calm veneer.

We were in my room at St. Margarita's, pretending to pore over study materials for math class. In reality, we were gazing from the window at the small sliver of lawn belonging to St. Benedict's, the boys' boarding school next door. That time of day, the lacrosse team would practice, and Pia and I would rate the players by their fuzzy silhouettes.

"Have you?" she prodded, sitting cross-legged on my bed.

I was on the floor, my math textbook opened in front of me. Using the pretense of reading it, I tried to disguise how I blushed.

Love was such a mystical, foreign concept back then. Something we both fantasized about with starry eyes and grandiose delusions of our future lovers.

"I hate it," Pia declared, and I looked up to find her twisting a silver ring around her finger, her gaze on the window. "We're told that it's supposed to feel wonderful, like magic. But it just makes you feel crazy. Like everything you thought made sense doesn't matter anymore. The entire world revolves around this one person. And they can decide to make it stop spinning whenever they want to. However, they want to. It's like they own you."

"That sounds cryptic," I joked, utilizing one of our English vocabulary words. So badly did I want to ask her more, but I'd remembered how she'd brushed off my earlier attempts to pry about her mystery man and backed down.

All I did was clear my throat and whisper, "What if it's not really love?"

"What?" Pia inclined her head, her beautiful lips pursed thoughtfully. "You'll never understand, Ada. You just don't know what it's like."

She gathered up her books then and left, calling over her shoulder as she entered the hall, "I'm going to hang with Alexi."

And I spent the rest of the night crying into my pillow, seething with jealousy.

But now...

I have to wonder just what she meant. Was she referring to my father then? Or someone else?

Who knows. Damn Domino for dredging up these old memories.

I never think of her this often. Certainly not twice in a handful of days. I've spent years smothering her ghost beneath a heap of repressed thoughts and subsequent trauma.

I will never admit it out loud, but her betrayal hurt me the worst, before Domino's, anyway. Such a beautiful, rare gem of a girl she was. So strong, so confident. She could empower a stone to come to life and speak with one of her smiles. She could have had any boy in a ten-mile radius with merely a wink and a nod.

Pia Inglecias could have had anyone she wanted.

She didn't need my father. She didn't have to prance around in outfits that—while modest—showcased her body's subtle curves and her tiny waist. She didn't have to be so damn beautiful, with eyes a mossy green and curling dark hair that framed a delicate face. She didn't have to carry herself with a maturity well beyond her fifteen years.

She didn't have to want him.

But she did. She used me to get to my father, and it was child's play for her. She thought she could manipulate the great and powerful Roy Pavalos.

And her plan worked—as long as my father was amused by her. Pia couldn't see it then, but she was only ever a toy to him. A playful distraction. A sick conquest.

Eventually, he grew tired of everyone. My mother. His two prior wives. Any piece of ass he took on the side.

They never held his interest for longer than a handful of minutes at a time. Why? Because Roy Pavalos only ever truly loved one person.

Himself.

If my father *did* kill Pia, then her diary alone wouldn't hold the answer—he would. Her final resting place would be a clever twist, a way for him to prove that he was always in control. His sick, twisted version of declaring the ultimate checkmate.

I could never think like him. I never understood his plots or his ploys. I only knew enough to play my role.

When it came to Pia, I was to lure her away and steal her diary.

But what if I was just seeing what he wanted me to see? A small piece in a much bigger plan…

Frustrated, I finally open my eyes, forsaking the past for the grim reality of my present circumstances. I can't tell how long I've been sitting here without a view of the sky, though my body is protesting in enough various aches and pains that I suspect at least an hour has passed.

Groaning with the effort, I disentangle myself from between the shelves and set my sights on the numerous items of hanging clothing. Alexi's familiarity with the wardrobe makes me suspect that, once again, Domino lied to me. He's had her here before, fucked her here, perhaps on that very bed he's regulated me to.

The thought sickens me, though I don't know why. I'm not jealous. I can't be. Domino Valenciaga, as I knew him is dead, and the monster holding me captive is a creature I want nothing to do with.

Though, for once, I'm willing to take a page out of my father's book. I can use him.

When I grab a dress, I put no thought into it, just picking the nearest item. I pull it on over my head without bothering to find any underwear to put on beneath.

My head held high, I finally leave the closet, only to realize that Alexi is gone. The room is drenched in darkness, proving my suspicion correct—it's already past nightfall. If I had to guess where Alexi might be, it's in Domino's bed right now, doing the very thing I told her to.

I shrug off the thought and make my way into the hall, moving blindly. I try to push everything else from my brain but the need to survive. Endure.

Domino dangled a sliver of freedom above my head, and I'd be a fool not to take it—though I don't trust him one damn bit. He'll screw me over in the end, I know that.

But not if I can screw him first.

As I near the door to his room, some of my resolve wavers. It's closed, and I can't help but wonder if the fact is a warning not to enter. Because he's busy fucking his toy. By breaching this boundary on my own, I'll only be asking to have that rubbed in my face.

So be it. I don't care about either of them enough to be offended. I'll be the daughter my father always wanted and refuse to give a damn about anyone but myself.

And, when it comes to survival, I'll do whatever it takes.

No matter how many times I feed myself that mantra, my fingers still shake as I grip the doorknob and twist, pushing the door open to a darkened room. My nostrils flare with Domino's scent, but to my surprise, I don't smell sweat or the fresh traces of sex.

Neither do I smell Alexi.

Straining my eyes, I blink through the shadows, and realize that the bed is empty. I feel along the wall for a light switch, revealing that, at a glance, the room itself seems deserted.

But no. *His* scent grows stronger the further I travel. Eventually, I venture far enough to see that the door to the balcony is open, letting in a wave of warm night air.

I don't check to see if he's there. Instead, I enter the closet, searching with a single-minded focus until I find what I'm after—Pia's diary.

I flip it open to a specific page and read while leaning against the cabinet full of watches, hearing them tick ominously in the background. The noise can't disguise the sound of his approach, however.

He's slow, lingering in the doorway with only the rasp of his breathing to give him away.

"Did I give you permission to go through that?"

I flinch but don't look up. In reality, I haven't been able to read a damn thing. At the sight of Pia's neat, deliberate handwriting, my vision blurred with the unmistakable burn of fresh tears.

I've missed her; how pathetic is that? All this time, I've held out hope that one day she would come out of the woodwork and explain where she'd been the last decade. Somewhere glamorous, of course. She would have amassed her own wealth somehow, and jet back into the city in a flashy sports car, her smile as charming as ever. Always bold, she'd seek me out without giving a damn about the rift between us.

Then she'd cajole her way back into my life, and things would go on as they used to be. When I felt like I had an ally outside of the carefully constructed world of Roy Pavalos.

But our friendship, much like everything else in my life, was nothing more than a well-crafted lie.

"Did you hear me?" He advances a step that has me sucking in a breath and jumping back before I can help it.

"D-Do you want my help or not?" I demand.

But then I make the mistake of looking up.

He hasn't been fucking Alexi—or if he has, their session was light enough that his hair has maintained the same shape our impromptu shower left it in—gently tousled around his shoulders.

He's left his chest bare, opting to wear only a pair of black slacks that don't look as though they've been hastily rebuttoned.

Not that I take comfort in the realization. Whether he's fucking Alexi or not is neither here nor there. All that matters is getting the leverage required to make him act on his word.

"Help," he echoes, his eyes flashing. For a second, I fear that I've misunderstood him all this time. Or that he's already grown bored of pretending to see me as anything more than a toy. "I don't remember asking for your help, Ada-Maria. I asked for answers."

A subtle warning that he won't accept anything but a concrete location when it comes to finding Pia's body.

Luckily for me, I think I may have an idea.

With his presence serving as a reminder of the threat looming over my head, I return my attention to the diary pages, this time seeing them clearly.

I'm on the right month, but the wrong day. Absently I flip toward the back of the diary, only to find that the week abruptly ends.

But not where it should.

I keep searching, scanning the remaining pages over and over until I notice a faint strip of ragged edges lining the binding.

"Some of the pages are missing," I blurt, raising my head to find Domino staring.

Rather than smug, or defensive, he looks… Confused. "If this is your way of trying to manipulate the situation, I would warn you to rethink that plan."

"I'm not. Look—" I shove the open book across the cabinet's glass surface.

Warily, he approaches, inspecting the journal himself. He frowns.

"Where did you get this?" I ask, recalling his vague answer the first time I asked this very question.

"Let's just say I found it," he says, still tracing the ragged edges of the pages. I know just from his clouded expression that he didn't realize they were missing at all. Which means they were torn out before he received it.

"Did you take it from my father?" I prod.

It's the most likely choice. After all, I personally gave him this diary, and I can attest that those remaining pages were there, though I barely remember what exactly they said.

I just know how angry they made me. How furious— enough so that I gave the journal to my father with no guilt.

At least, not then.

"Did you?" I ask when Domino doesn't reply.

His frown has deepened, his expression more guarded than ever. Finally, he sighs. "I got that book years before I even started working for Don Roy."

Some of my excitement deflates, replaced by even more confusion. "I… I don't understand."

"It's the truth," he counters. "But don't expect me to go on a wild goose chase, either." He takes a step in my direction, reinforcing the dangerous boundary between us. Captor and captive. "You've already read it, haven't you? So what the hell are you looking for?"

I ignore the question to phrase one of my own. "Did you read it?"

But he already confessed that he has.

"Then you know damn well that I wasn't lying. She was sleeping with my father."

And he knew that all along. It's why he started this vendetta against my family in the first place. Revenge.

But, again, his expression doesn't match. Instead of smug, he just looks cold. Impassive. Stone.

"I knew she was fucking someone," he says. "But nowhere in that journal does she write the name Roy. You know whose name she does write? Over and over, and over again? Yours—" He palms the counter with both hands, leaning across it so that his face is mere inches from mine. "Ada-Maria Pavalos. She wrote about how sneaky you were. How conniving. How much time the two of you spent together, and that you followed her around like a lost puppy—"

"Because she was using me," I rasp. "Duplicity and deception must run in the family."

He raises an eyebrow. "Respect for her is the only reason why I haven't slapped the taste out of your mouth," he warns in a tone so harsh I'm left reeling. He pushes back from the cabinet, turning for the main room. "I'm thinking I might rescind my offer—"

"I might know where to look," I rasp.

He stops over the threshold, his back to me. "If you think this is a game, I'm warning you. You don't want to play with me."

"I'm serious," I say. But hell, for all I know, this guess could be a wild shot in the dark. It's all I have. I'm not putting myself in Pia's shoes, though.

I'm thinking like my father. If I were a man like him with a secret to hide, where would I bury it?

It's obvious. Perhaps, *too* obvious. The consequences of being wrong are too dangerous to fathom, so I push all thought of failure from my mind and meet his piercing stare without flinching.

"I'm sensing you have the balls to tack a 'but' onto that statement," he murmurs.

"Y-Yes," I croak. His gaze is too intense; I have to tear my gaze away to the wall instead. Eyeing it, I find the strength to make a demand of my own. "*But,* I want something."

"And what is that?"

"I want proof that my father is dead."

He's silent for so long I risk a glance in his direction just to make sure he's still there.

He is, watching me with an unreadable expression. Finally, he inclines his head, running his hand along his jaw. "His smoking body cooking over an open spit wasn't proof enough for you?"

"I want a news article," I say, cringing. It's been hard enough trying to get those images from my mind. "The coverage must be wall to wall. Let me see it for myself, and that's all I'm asking for. Then, anything that I may know is yours."

As the seconds tick by—audibly, given his watch collection —I'm sure he'll refuse outright. Instead, he turns on his heel and reenters the room without a word.

I'm forced to follow him, catching him on the balcony, leaning casually against the railing as if he's enjoying the view.

"And?" I demand, my voice shrill.

"Give me a day." His tone is flat, betraying no hint of inflection. It's reminiscent of the chilling monotone he utilized as my father's trusted soldier doing God knows what for him day in and day out. Still, his acquiescence in this matter is something.

I'll take it.

"Thank you," I whisper, preparing to bolt back into that white room, regardless of if Alexi is there or not.

Before I can take a step, he turns, leveling me with the full weight of his icy stare. "You would thank the man who has your life in his hands? Don't be so eager, Ada. Your good girl act won't work here. I never promised I still won't sell you, did I?"

The dread I feel is like being drenched in ice water—a million different variations of shame and betrayal washing over me, one after the other.

Then I remember that I haven't told him anything. Either he stupidly revealed his whole plan to be a lie, or he's merely trying to rile me.

"I'm not eager," I counter, remaining within his orbit for a second longer despite every cell in my body urging me to run. "I'm earnest. Unlike you or my father, I am not a heartless, cruel excuse for a person, and I refuse to let you make me that way."

Rather than seem insulted, he laughs.

"So says the woman who fucks men with the same discernment most use when picking a public bathroom stall to use. You have no integrity. No shame. No honor."

"I have more honor than you do," I whisper harshly. "You act so high and mighty when you fucked Alexi. You've killed. You lied to me. You dragged me here, and you've hurt me. More than my father has, mind you. So don't you dare stare down your nose at me, Domino. You? You're evil—"

"You shut your fucking mouth about things you don't understand," he warns, pulling back from the railing to return to his full height.

"Or what?" I counter. My voice shakes so badly the words lack any confidence, but that's beside the point. I'm still here, standing as he advances with slow, heavy footsteps that radiate malice.

"Or..." He runs his fingers through my hair and cups the back of my skull in the same brutal motion. Swiftly, he yanks me toward him, nearly taking me off my feet. With our faces inches apart, he meets my gaze and holds it. "I'll teach you what evil truly is, Ada-Maria. Your father came as close to fitting the definition of that word as anyone I've ever met—but even he would shy from the things I've imagined doing to you."

I tremble at the pure, vicious intent in his voice. He means every word, and the gleam in his eyes seconds that. Whoever this man is now, he's not my father's trusty lackey or Pia Inglecias' long-lost brother.

He is a monster...

And I am at his mercy.

CHAPTER SEVEN

"I'm not talking about sex, either," he clarifies, lowering his gaze to my mouth. "You seem to enjoy that. I'll take pleasure in learning what it is you *don't* enjoy, as soon as I grow tired of hearing those pretty little moans of yours."

My cheeks sear, and the despair I feel is enough to drown me—but not yet. This time, I won't go down without a fight. I'll drag him down with me.

"You can do them," I rasp, "Whatever vile things you can come up with in that sick brain of yours—and know that with every vile act, I'll hate you more and more. Not that you'll care about that. But then you'll have to wonder, Domino. You'll have to compare every scream and cry to every night I've spent with you, and you'll realize just how damn good of an actress I am. Because every 'pretty little moan?' I've been faking them all this time. Why?" I force a laugh that has his nostrils flaring. "You truly believed that a brute like you could ever really get me off? Keep dreaming."

The lies assuage my aching pride, and his darkening expression makes toying with him in this way worth it. No matter how violent he is, or how much he claims to hate me, he's still susceptible to the same weakness as any other man.

Male pride.

"Sell me if you want to, you bastard," I add, hissing through my teeth. "At least then I might experience what a true orgasm is before I die—"

He grabs me by the throat, and I swear I see my entire life flash before my eyes. And what a sad, pathetic excuse for a life it truly was. Who was Ada-Maria Pavalos in the grand scheme?

Just a memory, the daughter of Roy. No one special enough to make her own mark on the world. Merely a tiny blip on a much bigger picture.

Men like Domino and my father make lasting impressions without even trying. They destroy the lives of those weaker, leaving destruction in their wake.

I wait for the violence in his touch—for the suffocating ache of my throat being crushed in his fist. Instead, he strokes his thumb along my windpipe as a lethal, gentle reminder of the damage he's capable of.

"So bold without your papa's shadow to hide behind, Ada-Maria," he taunts, but I can tell that beneath the mocking amusement is genuine curiosity. "That smart mouth has many hidden talents, though I strongly suggest that you reconsider which attributes might help extend your life a little longer."

"Why?" I ask in a tone that resembles a wail more. A whine. "I have nothing left to live for."

Except trying to preserve what small shreds of freedom I can claw back from him.

"You've taken everything."

"Everything?" The shift in his inflection is my only warning before he spins me around, putting my back to the railing. With his gaze boring directly into my own, he uses his grip on my neck to steer me back.

Back…

The metal rung digs into my lower back, but he keeps going, forcing me to bend against it. My heart lurches as I scramble for purchase, gripping the barrier on either side of me with both hands. Already, a sheen of sweat disrupts my grip—it will be child's play for him to shove me over entirely.

Kill me.

But, at least for now, his eyes lack any murderous intent.

"Everything?" he wonders softly. Viewing him from below, the harsh lines of his face are even more starkly beautiful in contrast to the way the moonlight glints off his skin. Soft, overhead light bathes everything on the terrace in a gentle, orange glow. The hue reflects off his eyes—he's on fire.

"There are so many things I deliberately haven't taken from you, Ada-Maria," he tells me. "Yet."

He releases my throat, and I writhe to pull myself upright. But he doesn't fully withdraw, forcing me to balance awkwardly, practically sitting on the railing while he blocks me in with his sheer bulk.

"Do you want to know why I put that feeding tube down your throat myself?" His eyes trace the line of my throat, skimming over my breasts to fixate on my heaving stomach. "Do you?"

His tone is persistent, though I'm too stunned by the abrupt change in subject to come up with a fitting answer. "W-What?—"

"I wanted you to have meat on that ass so that when I take you there, I'll have something to grab onto."

I blink, shocked by the coarse, blunt word usage as much as I am by his tone. Real emotion breaks through the level baritone, rousing a fear I've never felt before. He isn't angry or trying to scare me. He is dead serious.

"I needed you stronger," he adds, sliding his fingers against my jaw before cupping my entire cheek against his palm. "The things I have planned for you, Ada... You'll need all the strength you can get."

My mind goes blank as my fear builds to the point that I can taste it—fire, salt, and blood.

"First, you offer to save me," I croak. "And now, you threaten to hurt me."

"Don't sound so surprised." He drags his gaze up to mine, and I find his eyes devoid of a hint of sympathy or guilt. "I am a man of many talents," he confesses. "However, I never said that you wouldn't enjoy what I plan to do you. Oh no, Ada, I think you'll enjoy them very, very much. So much so that we can put your little theory to the test. How good of an actress are you?"

He laughs, leaning in so that his face is directly beside mine, his eyes on my throat.

"One could say I've become a connoisseur of the sounds made by Ada-Maria Pavalos over the years, and I have to admit that if you were faking, your acting skills have grown remarkably from over a month ago."

Was that the last time he watched some sordid recording of me?

I don't feed into his narrative outright. Instead, I meet his gaze and choke down the crippling unease warning me not to tangle with him. I should keep my mouth shut, or better yet, run.

Instead, I say, "What you think you heard, you'll never hear again. At least not in person. If you're still planning on selling me after all, then maybe you'll get lucky while I'm with my buyer. He might even let you watch."

His eyes narrow, and a jolt of alarm shoots down my spine. *Careful, Ada. You're on fragile ground.* "I don't think you'll enjoy making the sounds he'll wring from you, Ada-Maria."

He. The way he voices that word carries such vitriol that I know he's not referring to some nameless man in general. No, he has someone specific in mind.

Licking my lips, I hazard a guess, "Jaguar?"

"You…" Voice rumbling, he lowers his head, and his hair falls forward, shrouding his expression from view. "I think you'll want to be very careful with what you say next…"

I shiver, but I'm too tired to fight. The longer I maintain this precarious balance, the less fearful I feel. Why not just let him push me over? At least I'll be in control of my life for those final few seconds. No one can manipulate me anymore.

And yet, I can't resist one last jab, aiming to get under his skin any way I can.

"I'll ask him to record it for you," I murmur, arching my back, so that my mouth is near his ear this time. "And I'll make whatever damn sounds he asks me to."

He lunges.

A scream builds in my throat, but I don't even have the chance to voice it before he withdraws his support from me completely. I slip as my fingers lose their grip on the railing. In a heart-stopping jolt, I pitch backward.

At the same time, his hands latch onto my hips, anchoring me down. Rather than push me over, he sinks to his knees, wrenching my thighs apart.

A new kind of fear has me croaking, "D-Don't!"

Not that he heeds the refusal.

Unconcerned, he snatches up the hemline of my dress, exposing me to the warm night air. I shudder, trying to clamp my knees together, but he's too strong, utilizing brute force to keep them spread. Then his head lowers…

I squeeze my eyes shut, praying that he won't do what his position implies he might. Every muscle in my body goes rigid in grim anticipation as I feel his breath graze the innermost parts of me.

He breathes in. Out.

In and out.

I think he's toying with me on purpose, heightening the tension until it's electric. Unbearable. The folds of my pussy burn, exposed to his heat. Nerves explode, even without the aid of his touch. It's a cruel, pulsating sensation.

"S-Stop—"

"I could have you begging me to fuck you." His voice is a grated rasp—as if every word is being torn from the darkest parts of his brain. Those fantasies he's barely even aware of. "I could. I could have you screaming for me, gushing like a fucking geyser. I'd make you choke on every last word you've said."

The warmth basting my pussy turns hotter. Sweltering. I can't stop myself from writhing, wanting to pull away.

Get closer…

"But I won't." All at once, he stands, wrenching me down from my perch. His grip on my shoulder is the only force keeping me upright. My knees are wobbling, my legs jelly. "You want to know why? The world doesn't revolve around Ada-Maria's pussy."

He lets me go, forcing me to grapple for the railing to find my balance.

Dazed, I watch him re-enter the bedroom as his voice reaches back to me. "Decide if you plan to waste my time or not. You only have one chance to earn my trust. If not, I'll drag you to *Guarida del Tigre* myself, and believe me when I say that I will watch, Ada-Maria. But I don't think you'll enjoy yourself half as much as you seem to think you will. Jaguar's world won't be as kind to you as mine has."

When he's gone, the impact of his words resonates like a gut punch. Dejected, I sink to my knees, still gripping the balcony, my eyes on the shadowed landscape below. I'm terrified of what might await me; I truly am.

I'm more terrified, however, by the prospect of what his "protection" entails. Something tells me that Domino Valenciaga has a warped concept of the phrase. The last thing on earth I should strive to gain is his trust.

And yet…

I don't have a choice.

It's either him or the unknown, and—at least for now—I'd rather take him.

If only to be the one to push him figuratively overboard in the near future.

CHAPTER EIGHT

I wake up in the white room, startled and disoriented. For one, I don't remember how I got here. I have no recollection of leaving Domino's room…

In fact, my last memory is huddling on the balcony, still stung from his taunt.

For now, I put the mystery out of my mind and sit upright, realizing that I'm lying on the bed, atop the neatly made sheets.

Alexi isn't anywhere in sight, at least. Golden sunlight bathes the room in warm shades of yellow that cast a chilling background to the tension still lingering in the air. Domino isn't around either, but he's close. I can sense him and his rage smoldering somewhere within the house, waiting to descend.

I'll make him wait a little longer, though.

I enter the closet and strip my black dress in favor of a new one. This style is lighter, made out of white cotton, and breathable in the heat. When I return to the bed, I find that someone must have come in without me realizing it, leaving a silver tray on the bed. Ines?

I barely pay the food a passing glance, but something catches my eye. A square, white envelope strategically placed upright against a plate of scrambled eggs and beautifully arranged fruit. My name is written across it in sloping handwriting.

Cautiously, I open it, finding just a plain white card with a message written on it. While Ines may have left this tray for me, I doubt she penned these two lines in menacing black script.

I suggest you eat. Or you will regret it.

A friendly morning missive from Domino.

I rip it in half, letting the pieces fall at my feet. Then I turn my back on the tray, fully intending not to eat so much as a damn bite. Let him make his demands and pose all the threats he wants.

But then I realize that I would only be giving him an opening to escalate his taunts. My stomach drops as I remember what happened on the balcony. Every time I try to meet him tit for tat, he turns the tables.

Ignoring him now would be a blatant invitation for him to impose yet another change to our dynamic. Perhaps try to do more than shove a feeding tube down my throat, for instance.

I shudder at the prospect and wind up sitting on the edge of the bed before I can rethink my options. I grab a fork, stab at a piece of egg and bite it, chewing mechanically.

The taste barely registers, but the sickening sensation of food filling my stomach is unbearable. I nearly spit it out. The need to purge is so damn overwhelming that it takes effort to swallow. Once I do, I drop the fork, lurching to my feet.

I've done enough.

But then I picture his expression as he said, "You'll need your strength." In reality, he likes me weak and powerless. He prefers having the utmost control over my body and my life.

He'd love having one more reason to rip away what fragile autonomy I have left.

So I force myself to pick up the fork and take another bite. And another.

The food feels like lead going down my throat, but with every subsequent bite, I can't ignore the selfish satisfaction I feel at denying him a victory in this arena. He'll have to look for something else to lord over me, another weakness to exploit. I won't let him play on my insecurities so recklessly.

Fuck him.

I surprise myself and nearly clear the entire plate. I even manage to consume most of the fruit, and when I finally step back from the tray, I'm grinning. For the first time in years, a full stomach doesn't make me feel disgusting and stuffed.

I feel ready to face him and whatever he might throw at me next.

But the second I step one foot beyond the doorway, that bravery fades. I'm on his turf again, forced to navigate his twisted, dark world without any sense of direction.

It's still morning, I think. When I head for the circular foyer that serves as the heart of the house, a rare sound reaches my ears, so disarming that I stop in my tracks and crane my head to listen.

Laughter. Sexy, raucous laughter—a female and a male's, his deep and melodic and unmistakably genuine.

I'm skeptical as I gather up the nerve to follow it, convinced that a different man must be out on the terrace where the sound resonates the strongest. Perhaps the mysterious Jaguar returned to see our dynamic in action for himself?

But no.

The figure chuckling shamelessly on a white lounger, his head thrown back to expose his throat, is Domino Valenciaga, Alexi seated across from him.

"I told you," she purrs, leaning toward him so that her ample breasts threaten to spill from her low-cut white tank top. "I am a woman of many talents."

"I believe you," Domino replies. "It takes a certain talent for attracting trouble to catch Jagger's attention."

"Oh no you don't," Alexi teases. "No prying, Dom. It's rude."

She doesn't see me, smirking at him, her blue eyes sparkling.

But he does. He goes silent mid-laugh, and even I can admit that the shift in him is terrifying to witness. His eyes lose what hint of warmth they had and go cold as his shoulders fall into a hard, rigid line. With a stern tilt of his chin, he levels his gaze in my direction.

God, he must truly hate me. It's the only explanation for why he can react to me so harshly within seconds.

And yet, while alone with Alexi, display a relaxed demeanor I don't think I've ever seen him embody. Not once during my captivity, not even during all the years he worked for my father. In fact…

I don't think I've ever heard him laugh like that.

"I need to speak to Ada-Maria in private," he says. His chilling tone spurs Alexi to lurch to her feet without argument. Swaying her hips, she heads inside, staring right past me, her nose in the air. I ignore the slight and focus on the man before me.

He's leaning forward, his hands braced on either knee like a soldier readying for battle. His outfit reinforces that comparison. He's swapped the dark attire for white today, opting for slacks and a loose shirt—but, for what I think is the first time, he's left the buttons completely undone.

Given the fact that Alexi didn't seem bothered by the sight of his scar, I realize that it wasn't modesty or shame that drove him to cover it all this time. It was me.

He didn't want me to see it, and I doubt that fear of my reaction was his motive. He wanted to make sure that he held all the cards at his disposal until the last possible second, shielding his supposed identity as Pia's brother.

Which means that he doesn't think I'm quite as stupid as he pretends.

"Morning. Did you enjoy your breakfast?" he asks, his tone flat in comparison to his laughter.

I force a smile in return. "It was marvelous. I was starving, thank you."

I see his eyebrow go up, and I get the sense that he's wrestling with storming into my room and seeing the tray for himself. Instead, he snaps his fingers, and a woman appears in the doorway, too short to be Alexi.

"Ada-Maria is done with her breakfast, Ines," Domino says, which I assume is her cue to go check.

In the meantime, he nods toward the lounger Alexi vacated.

"Have a seat."

I deliberately skip over the lounger he indicates, claiming the one slightly further apart, just beyond his reach.

His eyes narrow at the insolence. To my shock, though, he doesn't call me out directly. Instead, he sits back, crossing his arms to inspect me with a searching glance that has me squirming.

"I'll give you one last chance to rethink lying to me," he says, his voice soft and nonthreatening—which just makes me even more on edge. I don't trust this suddenly patient side of him. A threat lurks beneath it, I'm sure of that. "Admit now that you were playing a game, and when I whip you in punishment, I'll do so gently."

The genuine excitement in his voice chills me to the core—though it shouldn't. Hurting me is one of the few things that seems to arouse Domino Valenciaga.

That, and when I dare to step toe to toe with him and play devious mind games of my own.

"And if I'm not lying?" I counter, lifting my chin to hold his gaze unflinchingly. "What will I win?"

His teeth flash in a dangerous smile, his laughter coarse, echoing throughout this part of the terrace. "You'll earn time," he says. "Trust me, that's the most precious commodity you can attain at a moment like this."

Because he's the one who decided to leverage my "time" in the first place by selling me. He's the monster in this equation—I can't forget that.

Even if I have to pretend to make nice with him long enough to earn as many precious seconds as I can.

"I think I know where you can start looking," I say, phrasing my wording carefully. I'm not outright claiming to know where Pia's body is—or if she's really dead. But if he hopes to find something, I'm the best option he has.

All I have to do is see the world from Roy Pavalos' cruel, calculated viewpoint. Where most men would see a plain, featureless map, my father would see territory ripe for the taking and various features to exploit.

As long as he worked for him, I'm sure Domino knows exactly how his old boss used to operate. He wouldn't demand an answer from me if he didn't think I was capable of coming up with one, either because my father told me or because I happened to guess.

Aware of that, his sly grin falls.

"I'm the best chance you have," I say, risking provoking him by prodding his weakness outright. I can't help it. For once, I have some semblance of an upper hand.

For a heartbeat, of course.

A second later, he's on his feet, approaching me slowly. I shiver as he places one hand on my shoulder. His fingers flex, teasing me with a fraction of his strength, a mere reminder of the damage he's capable of.

"Don't think you can jerk me around, Ada-Maria," he warns, using that same hand to brush a stray curl from my cheek. "I could kill you right now, and never even have to justify why I changed my mind." He strokes a path up to sink his fingers through my hair, capturing a handful of it. Brutally, he yanks, so hard that tears spring to my eyes. "Understand?"

"Again, you keep hinting that you have no intention of honoring your own offer," I croak, blinking back unwanted tears. Gradually, he releases the pressure, still keeping his hand against my skull. "Why should I even trust you?"

His nostrils flare, his eyes darkening as if he's mulling over the prospect of humoring me at all. *Too far, Ada*, a part of me warns. *You can't push him too far.*

My only hope is to reel him back.

"I want to trust you," I force myself to whisper. The words fall flat, nowhere near convincing.

And yet, he laughs, amused all the same.

"I love the way you look when you try your mind games on me." He lets me go and moves to stand near the balcony, gazing at the gardens below. "You get this pathetic, hopeful glint in your eyes. It's fucking sexy. If I were a dumb cunt like the other men you've fucked." This time the warning in his voice rings out loud and clear. "Don't make the mistake of thinking I am. For your sake, Ada-Maria."

"I won't," I rasp, though I think I'm speaking to myself more than him. I can't keep getting caught up in his game. I need to stay one step ahead. "So what if I do know where she is, Pia? Do you have proof that my father is dead?"

With his back to me, I only have his posture from which to discern his reaction. But it's… Alarming. He stiffens in a way that has me bolting to my feet, readying for an assault from his end at any moment. I hate these volatile shifts in him. They're like a storm that comes on suddenly with no warning.

"Proof," he echoes in an unsettlingly deep tone. "Should I have his body dug up for you, Ada? The pieces, anyway. Or dissect the dogs I had the rest of his remains fed to? I'm sure you thought out exactly how you might be presented with such evidence?"

I'm winded by the grisly images. At the same time, I'm resigned, almost anxious to see them. Anything. It won't be real until I know for sure.

Only then can I truly grieve.

Or dread the possibility that he's been lying to me all along.

Without revealing an answer either way, he heads toward the archway leading inside the house. I start to panic, worried he's about to turn the tables yet again. Leave me waiting.

Instead, he cocks his head, my sole warning to follow.

Eagerly, I trail him through the foyer, past my room, and into his. In neither space do I find any sign of Alexi. Is she still here?

I don't have the strength to ask. He demands my sole focus, and every brain cell in my skull is consumed with him.

I hold my breath as he approaches the bed. Will sex be the next hurdle I'll have to jump through?

No. He reaches past the rumpled sheets for a nightstand made of dark wood. From it, he grabs a small, electronic device that I'm sure wasn't there before. He had it ready for this moment. Waiting.

"Here—" He hands the object to me—a small tablet with a video already pulled up on the screen. A white play button lurks over a still shot of what looks like a reporter in a newsroom. "Watch it."

My finger shakes as I tap the screen, triggering the video to play.

Within seconds, I get my answers as to my father's fate.

"Tragedy in Terra Rodea, as more details about a fatal crash involving mayoral candidate Roy Pavalos and his wife Lia, who was declared dead on the scene. Mr. Pavalos has been transferred to a local hospital where he's still listed in critical condition…"

Thud! My knees hit the floor as the tablet falls from my grasp, clattering across the polished marble. It all comes back to me. All of the fear, and the pain, and the uncertainty.

Like a punch, the revelations slam into me, and I sob louder with each one.

My mother is dead, beautiful and sweet and innocent in the grand scheme of my father's empire. I haven't let myself think of her until now—I couldn't. She wasn't perfect…

But the loss of her guts me. I'm hollowed by the thought of never seeing her again. Never having her presence as a buffer against my father's criticism.

Because he's still alive.

Roy Pavalos is still alive.

And I wish Domino would have killed me himself.

CHAPTER NINE

I don't know how long I lie here, screaming and screaming. Eventually, he must leave and return because everything goes cold all at once. Wet.

Sputtering, I realize that he threw something on me. Water? It's cold enough to suck the air from my lungs, rendering me silent in an instant. My mouth is still open though, making noises that scratch from my throat, robbed of all intensity.

"You will have plenty of time to mourn later," Domino warns in a voice so cold the liquid dripping off me feels scalding in comparison.

I watch, numb, as he sets an empty glass pitcher onto the same nightstand he took the tablet from. With his back to me, he rakes a hand through his hair, and I can sense the irritation prickling beneath his skin. This is restraint from him, I realize.

Because in reality, he wants to do a whole lot more than douse me with ice water.

The full extent of his cruelty—and his hate—feels dizzying to examine in full, now that I have video evidence. My father may not be dead, but in so many ways…

The truth is far worse.

"She loved you," I croak, once I find my voice again. It sounds like such a childish thing to say, but it's the truth. I think of my mother and how much she struggled over the past few months. A struggle I did everything in my power to ignore, from drinking myself into a daze to resorting to cocaine. I denied her when she needed me the most.

Selfishly, I think. Because I assumed she already had someone to help her through that pain, someone more reliable than I ever could be. As much as he may deny it, Domino ran errands for her when he thought no one was looking—but I always had my eyes on him and never missed the days he'd take her prescriptions to the pharmacy. The nights he'd escort her from dinner when the exhaustion became too much. I used his loyalty to her to justify my indifference.

And he killed her.

"Why?" Tears lash at my vision, blinding me to everything, even common sense. Somehow I'm on my feet, launching myself toward him—but I don't even touch him before he pivots, shoving me onto the bed.

"This shouldn't be a shock to you, Ada-Maria," he points out. "I've told you the truth from the start."

He has. Maybe, all this time, despite his taunts, I truly didn't believe it.

"Why Mama?" I rasp. "She was a good person. She never hurt anyone. She—"

"She left you at the mercy of a tyrant for your entire life, Ada. Don't make her out to be a saint," he scolds, but his tone falls flat. He's merely saying those words, but they lack the hatred of when he speaks of my father, or even me.

"Why?"

"Why do you think, Ada?" His tone turns cutting and harsh. "She had terminal cancer, was taking enough pain medication to fell a horse, and she suffered the trauma of a 'car crash.' A papercut could have killed her at this point. Crying changes nothing. It happened."

"But my father…"

That news report must be from days ago, I realize. Probably the same night I was abducted. If my father was in the hospital in critical condition, I doubt Domino would have been able to obtain his body in time to roast over an open spit.

"Still in critical condition," Domino says, now facing the windows that portray storm clouds moving across the horizon. "Last I heard, the bastard is still peeing out of a tube and breathing with the aid of some very expensive machinery. The DA is still hot on his ass, though. He'll be in for a rude awakening, dead or not—"

"So… You lied."

I'm on my feet again, and this time I feel my palm connect with his shoulder hard enough to sting.

"You bastard!"

He doesn't waste effort to restrain me this time. He merely turns, leveling me with the full brunt of a glare so chilling I stagger back in the face of it.

"Tell me, Ada, are you truly this gullible? Sometimes, I will admit that it is hard to tell."

"You're sick." I'm sobbing in earnest, barely able to get the words out completely. The full breadth of his lies is mind-numbing. Insane. And twisted. "Who was that?" I demand, swaying on my feet. I have to brace most of my weight against the nearest wall just to stay upright. "On the spit?"

"Oh, that?" he shrugs as if I asked him about the brand of clothing he's wearing. "That was a clever arrangement of pork. Very convincing if I say so myself."

Too convincing. It strikes me that I honestly don't know which is the lie.

My head is spinning, my throat constricting. The food from earlier jolts in my stomach, heavy and repulsive.

Purge.

The impulse is so strong that I'm already racing into the hall by the time he catches me, looping an arm around my waist. His strength imbibes that limb with the sturdiness of an iron bar, driving every ounce of air from my chest in one blow.

I wheeze, finding myself slung into the air, my legs kicking helplessly at nothing.

"Oh no, you don't," Domino growls, his voice emanating somewhere near my head.

I blink, finding that the floor is whizzing by below me, but I'm suspended against a firm, moving surface heading swiftly in the direction of his bedroom.

"No," he repeats, dropping me without warning.

I brace myself for a brutal impact and land on something soft instead. The bed. Scrambling for purchase, I watch him approach the door and slam it shut.

When he faces me…

It's like my brain flips some internal switch. Anger gives way to a terror unlike any I've ever felt. It's all-encompassing and draining, leaving me slumped on my side as he advances.

"I won't let you play the hysterical victim, Ada," he says coldly. "Scream. Cry. Commence with your fake mourning —*after* you give me what you promised."

Fake mourning.

"She was my mother," I croak, my face still damp with tears. Fresh ones continue to fall, dripping from my jaw onto my collar. If I close my eyes, I could imagine them to be droplets of blood.

Though in all honesty, this is no different. I'm bleeding in a way that feels as real as if I'd been stabbed through the chest. Some of it is shock, I think.

To really see her smiling photo paired with that tragic headline. That makes it so much more real than having him taunt me with her death.

It hurts.

But if I'm being honest with myself, I'd admit that some of this emotion stems from another source entirely, one more primal than pain and love.

It's fear.

My father is still alive, and yet Domino has kept me here for over a week without anyone coming for me. It doesn't make sense.

It feels so much more unsettling than being faced with what I presumed to be his body, turning on a spit. Roy Pavalos is never caught off guard, never. He is never without a plan or some kind of insurance policy to make sure that, no matter what, he comes out on top.

What the hell has Domino unleashed?

And why?

"Did you hear me, Ada-Maria?" His voice intrudes on my thoughts, and I blink to find him watching me with an intensity that puzzles me more than the fact that my father is still alive.

"W-What?"

"Where is the body?"

Whose body? is my initial response. Then I remember…

Pia.

I promised to give him a place to look.

"In hell," I snarl. "Where all of you belong!"

It's the wrong thing to say. I don't even see him move before my throat is between both of his hands, crushed like a stress ball.

I see stars. Death feels so imminent that I don't even have the chance to feel the full extent of the fear I should be experiencing. I just stare up at the ceiling, waiting for my vision to finally cut out once and for all.

But he merely intended the violence to serve as a warning. Barely a second passes before he releases some of the pressure, allowing me to choke down the minimum amount of air to stay conscious.

"Think carefully, Ada," he cautions. His voice shakes, betraying just how close he is to losing control. I've never heard him like this.

Unstable. Enraged. Unpolished.

"Give me what you promised, or I swear to God you will regret it. Your mother will soon become a distant memory, because I will put you through a living hell before sending you to meet her. Do you understand?"

I do. His voice alone conveys as much. He means every word he's saying; I can't deny that. Even as I pull back far enough to see his handsome face sculpted by rage, bathed in the gray overcast light filtering in from the windows.

I can see understanding dawn across those very features as I open my mouth and spit at him.

Wham! One moment I'm on the bed; the next, I'm on the cold, hard floor in a place that I sense isn't the main bedroom. The lighting is different here, the flooring polished enough to display my reflection in pitiful relief.

I'm shaking; my eyes resemble black holes; they're so swollen. But my appearance is nowhere near as frightening as that of the man looming over me.

He waits until I look at him before he moves, crossing over to an oval-shaped tub paces away. We're in the bathroom, I realize with a start.

Which means…

I see his arms strain as he wrenches on the faucet, sending the water streaming into the tub's basin. Somehow, I can easily read his intentions. It's like our minds are in sync, one and the same. I know exactly what he intends to do.

Kill me.

Kill me slowly.

Run! I scramble onto my hands and knees, my eyes on the door.

He's already gaining on my position before I can even make a move. Cruelly, his hand latches onto a chunk of my hair, using it to drag me across the room to the tub. Then he yanks me onto my knees, forcing me to bend over the rim as the water churns below.

I can't even suck in air before I'm submerged. The shock is more terrifying than the fact that I can't breathe. All I can do is fight with everything I have.

I feel my legs kick against the floor as my fingers claw at his hand, nails scraping against his flesh.

He's too strong. When my head is suddenly wrenched above the water's surface, it's entirely of his own will. I might as well be a gnat fighting against a mountain.

"Where is she?"

I sputter, more intent on breathing than compiling an answer.

With a growl, he shoves me down, and I'm under again.

Never, in my life, have I felt anything like this. My pulse is a thundering beat hammering through my eardrums, my lungs on fire, every nerve screaming, on red alert.

And yet, internally, somewhere in between his next vicious reprieve as he yanks me above the water, I realize that there's no point in fighting. Let him win this round.

So, I make myself so limp he doesn't seem prepared to resist.

"Shit!"

His voice echoes in tandem with a sickening *thunk!* Pain washes through my skull as pressure fills my nostrils. But this doesn't feel like drowning.

It hurts too damn much. But then a flood of warm, hot liquid spills over my face, filling my nose and seeping into my mouth. He must be pouring it onto me, I realize, because I'm staring up at the ceiling now, choking on the substance that my brain belatedly identifies. Something far too thick to be water…

Blood.

"Ada, shit—" He grabs me, hauling me upright. This time, his method of suffocation comes in the form of a delicate, white substance that he presses frantically against my nose. "Tilt your head! I said, tilt your fucking head up!"

I obey him solely on impulse, the need to breathe outweighing all else. My mouth is open, though, gulping at the air, despite the pressure on my nostrils. He's holding them both shut, forcing my head back against his shoulder.

Frantically, my gaze darts around him, trying to discern the source of the substance still dripping down my face. Blood.

So much blood. I'm covered in it, and droplets of red speckle the floor.

"Why the hell did you do that?" His voice echoes off the walls, losing its emotionless cadence. Rage and confusion add color to his tone, enhancing his mysterious accent and giving his baritone a threatening timbre it usually lacks. "You'll be lucky if you didn't break your fucking nose—"

"I hate you." It feels important to say that despite everything else.

He has me on his lap, I think, his legs sprawled over the floor beneath me. One of his hands loops around me from behind so that he can hold the tissue to my nose, while the other has both of my wrists in an iron grip.

To stop me from slapping him.

"I hate you."

"I know," he says, monotone once more. His chest rumbles against my back as he speaks, his breath on my ear, his grip unwavering.

"I will never forgive you for this." A sob edges my words. I sound like a child, wailing and desolate.

"You won't," he agrees, forcing my chin even higher.

My nose is the source of the bleeding; I can tell now. I must have hit it off the tub. It throbs, sending pain lancing through my skull with every beat of my heart. Is it broken?

How fitting if it is. He took my mother away, my family, my life.

Why not take my beauty, too? It's the only thing of value I ever had, and it's somehow managed to outlast the other bastions of my life as a Pavalos. What use am I without my father to control my every movement and my mother to lurk obliviously in the background, pretending that she doesn't realize the hell we're both living under?

"I hate you—"

"So hate me, then," Domino commands, sounding in control once more. Still, he applies even more pressure to my nose, forcing me further against his chest. "Hate me all you want, Ada… I can allow you that much."

More tears spill down my cheeks, mingling with the blood. This is his idea of mercy—doling out hate as though it's a cherished gift. The only thing he can and will ever offer me.

Hate and pain.

And lies.

CHAPTER TEN

He goes away. I'm so numbed by exhaustion that I don't even recall when or why. I'm still lying on the bathroom floor, facing the tub, surrounded by a graveyard of crumbled, blood-stained tissue.

It took several tries before the bleeding stopped completely. My nose feels like a swollen, painful lump that hurts to breathe through. I try running my finger along its bridge to assess the damage and wind up moaning, seeing stars that speckle my vision.

"You didn't break it."

I stiffen with the realization that Domino is still here, just somewhere beyond my line of sight, his voice effortlessly resonating throughout the entire room.

"You'll live."

It's a mean choice of words, and I can't help but laugh at them. However, the sound comes out resembling a sob more.

"You are nothing like Pia," I tell him. Considering everything Pia Inglecias put me through, that isn't a compliment. A teenage girl who used lies and manipulation to get her way, still possessed more tact and humanity than he has.

I think of them in comparison to each other, and I can't even discern a physical resemblance. Except for their eyes, maybe. Both have that same, murky hue of hazel, though the green in Pia's was more prominent.

She was so very beautiful. That beauty aided in her confidence and ability to win anyone over to her side. She had a way of making someone feel special, like the most important person in the world, just as long as they had her attention. She could be so sweet when she wanted to and so damn charming.

On the other hand, when the mood struck her, she could be so very mean.

"I'll keep that in mind," Domino replies, and his voice alone reinforces the divide between him and my childhood friend. Pia spoke musically, her emotions evident in her tone. When she was happy, she almost sounded as though she were singing. When she was angry, her words became honed like a whip, lashing out at whatever had sparked her ire.

"I don't think my father killed her," I admit, though I don't know if I'm speaking to myself more than Domino.

Why would he kill her? She was everything I could never be, a perfect missing key to his arsenal of manipulation and influence. He could have molded Pia under his wing, using her to do whatever he desired. Not just sexually, but politically.

She would have served him far better than I ever could.

Killing her would be messy. It would mean utilizing his precious resources and covering his tracks. Doable, but requiring far more effort than I think a schoolgirl with a crush would demand. Even if she went public about her relationship with my father, it would be her word against his.

And his word was law.

"But if he did," I add, my voice scratching at the silence. "He would need a reason..."

Something more egregious than her simply stealing money from him. She would have needed evidence of something far more damaging. So damaging, in fact, that nothing plausible comes to mind. This isn't some scripted crime drama. My father was a violent, egotistical, misogynistic man, but he wasn't pure evil.

Though, I guess I should use present tense, considering that he's still alive…

"I have reason to believe that Pia had something that would put his entire future into question," Domino admits. "More than money. Something that would cast a shadow on him not just politically, but make him a walking target of his most powerful enemies."

I frown, triggering a wave of pain that spreads from my nose and into my eye sockets. I let my eyelids lower and contemplate such a possibility in the darkness. If his reputation was on the line…

Well, that was something that Don Roy would kill to protect. He'd do anything to shield his image, no matter the cost.

Anything.

"What was it?" I ask.

Only silence comes in response. I start to question if he's still here, but I can sense his presence, as vibrant as the blood. He must be behind me, lurking by the door, blocking my potential exit should I gather the nerve to stand.

I'm too tired to move at all, and I contemplate drifting off here and now. Let him wallow in his hate and self-pity. Let him go on a wild goose chase after rumors and a ghost.

And yet, I can't deny a prickle of curiosity strong enough to make me peel my eyes open again.

"Do you even know?"

"I know," he says with a certainty that irritates my already frazzled nerves. He's not lying—and I hate that. It gives him some tiny semblance of a right to hate my family all this time. If my father really did kill Pia, he would deserve far worse than a car crash.

But what about me?

I'm guilty too, I decide, shying from those memories. Anything that happened to her would be squarely my fault.

"If he… She'll be in Terra Rodea," I say, voicing my fragile hunch.

"Damn it, *that's* all you have?" He scoffs. "If that's a guess, Ada, I would have expected something with more effort. Do you think if she were still in the city, she wouldn't have been found by now within the past ten years? I would assume he'd dump her in a swamp, or a lake, or on one of your family's vacation homes—"

"He'd keep her in Terra," I insist. With what little strength I can muster, I roll onto my side, groaning at the pain. I'm panting when I finally turn to face him. As I suspected, he's leaning against the closed door to the balcony, his arms crossed, eyes narrowed.

"So you were bullshitting me all along—"

"He would keep her in Terra," I say over him, surer of that than ever. I may not have learned much in my life, but I know my father. I've gotten a taste of the way he thinks and how he moves. How he likes to gloat and lord himself over the things he believes he owns, be them places, objects, or even people. "Why do you think I stayed there?" I demand when Domino's expression remains skeptical. "Why do you think he kept me in that house, by him always?"

It wasn't out of the devotion of a caring father, though I think Domino knows that already. A grudging expression crosses over his face. I have his attention. For now.

And I don't waste it.

"He would keep her somewhere close, but within plain view. A place he could always have access to but somewhere that couldn't be directly traced to him. Not a vacation house or one of our properties, either. That would be too obvious."

And I'm sure that there are no dead bodies buried on our property. My father could be cruel, but he was never sloppy.

"If I had to guess, I would narrow it down to a handful of places," I add, though I rationalize even telling him this by reminding myself that I don't believe it. Nothing—short of his own mortal soul—would be worth the risk. Pia wasn't some political rival or a lawless cartel leader. She was a fifteen-year-old girl with a family, and people who loved her enough to mount a search.

I remember seeing the flyers. I remember hearing word of her mother's anxious search. I remember that a broken heart was rumored to be the cause of death when Rosa Inglecias collapsed four months into her daughter's disappearance.

"Where?" Domino demands, letting his hands fall to his sides. His fingers twitch impatiently, and I suspect it's taking restraint on his part to keep from lunging at me and wringing out an answer. "If the bastard would be stupid enough to bury her in Terra, then where?"

"His office," I say, naming one of three potential locations.

"Where would he bury her?" Domino counters. "Under the elevator?"

He's right. I haven't had time to consider the logistics in full. They're just guesses of the places I know my father values and frequents.

"One of the parks he had dedicated around the city, then?"

"The earliest one wasn't erected until two years after Pia went missing," Domino says, proving that he's considered these options already. He's obsessed over them, I realize as he starts to pace, wearing a frown reminiscent of the one he'd sport all those nights when I'd watch him on my family's property. "Where else? Tell me you have a better guess than that."

The final one I've considered the least. It would be the most unlikely of all, I can admit that. And yet…

It would be the cruelest.

"The old Inglecias house," I croak.

Domino stops mid-stride, his foot still hovering in the air. I can tell from how his eyes widen that he hasn't considered that location for himself.

"No," he says, shaking his head. "That would be fucking stupid. Why would he…"

"Because it would be so obvious," I point out. A hollow laugh escapes me at the thought of how he would have gloated, were any of this true. "My father was… Is a selfish victor, Domino. Don't tell me you haven't realized that. He guards his prizes jealously."

My mother.

Me.

He wouldn't see Pia as a person, or even an innocent victim who got in his way. He would only see her as a prize to be won. Or conquered.

"He would keep her in Terra," I decide, ignoring his skeptical frown. "Not that I believe he did it in the first place."

I can't tell if Domino agrees with me or not. He's still pacing, raking his fingers viciously through his hair. He has to be hurting himself, ripping out stray strands with each frantic motion, but I don't think he notices. Or cares. Wherever he is mentally is somewhere beyond pain or discomfort.

"Fuck," he says finally, moving to brace his hands against the counter. He eyes himself in the mirror positioned above, and from this angle, I can see his expression clearly.

Angry. Bitter. Thoughtful.

As much as he may have challenged it, I think my hunch made sense.

Which sickens me to my very core.

"And this is the part where you laugh like a superhero villain," I croak, too drained to put any real effort into the taunt. My head lolls, and I find myself staring at the shower instead of him. "Then you tell me that it was all a trick. You'll leave me to die. I was an idiot to even think of trusting you—"

"I'll uphold my end of our agreement," he snarls, marching to cross my line of vision. "I'll *trust.*' But can you?"

I blink, puzzled by his statement.

His expression shifts before my eyes, becoming musing again, reminding me more than ever of those nights I would spy on him. He's thinking. Plotting. And this time, whatever he's planning most definitely involves me.

"I'll need to do this right," he grumbles, stroking his chin, fixated on his own internal thoughts. He's not speaking to me. And yet, as his eyes dart suspiciously around the room, I suspect that I'm not who he's wary of, either. At least now. "Get up."

He lowers his voice and inclines his head toward the shower stall.

But I don't move.

"I said get up!" He storms toward me, his nostrils flaring. One look at me, however, and he seems to realize that my rebellion isn't entirely out of a need to defy him.

I can't move. My head is floating, my body like lead.

Without a word, he crouches, yanking me into his arms. I barely have the chance to marvel at the sensation of being held by him—carried—before I'm unceremoniously placed on one of the benches in the shower stall.

He exits long enough to get the water running, but this time the spray is heavy, pelting us with lukewarm water that ricochets off the walls in a deafening roar.

"Trust is what you want, is it?" Domino questions, his voice low as he returns to my side, bringing his mouth near my ear. "Keep your mouth shut, follow my lead, and I'll do what I can to help you."

Help me?

It takes every ounce of strength I have left to find the energy to lift my head and see his face. He's leaning down, still wearing his shirt and slacks, and I realize that all of this is a way to disguise our conversation.

From who? Alexi?

But in comparison to him, even she no longer seems like my biggest enemy.

"You did this to me!" I'm on the verge of another sob, and he nods, tugging me from the bench and onto my feet. I sway, forced to submit to his strength just to stay upright. He hooks an arm around my waist, and I have no choice but to brace my hands against his chest for stability.

"I did this to you," he murmurs. "But do you want to learn why? Or would you rather wallow in your role as the victim?"

I recoil at his harsh tone, pushing against him. Belatedly, I realize just what he said—learn. It's the first time he's even hinted at giving me more than taunts and mind games. God help me; I'd do anything for answers. Clarity. Something.

Even if it means humoring him a second longer.

"What do you mean?"

"This was always bigger than you," he tells me. "Bigger than us. If you want any prayer of getting out of this alive, I'm the only shot you have. Do you understand that? Ines can't help you. Not Alexi, not your father. No one but me."

He's still speaking softly. But that does nothing to diminish the seriousness in his tone.

"Then tell me why."

He pulls back, forcing me to stand on my own. "I will," he says, turning to brace his hands against the hard, granite before him. "But if I do, you will no longer have the luxury of doubting me. This isn't a game, Ada-Maria. The stakes are higher than you could ever imagine."

"You keep dancing around the truth," I point out, approaching him only because I need the support of the wall just to stay upright. I lean against it, closing my eyes as the water continues to pelt us both. I can feel the steam rising, enclosing us in a false layer of privacy. We're in our own twisted realm now, just him and I.

And I should be busy finding a way out. Not listening to him.

"Speak, or I swear to God, Domino, I'll…"

"You have four more days." He says it with such malice that I shrink inside myself, picturing what lurks at the end of that timeframe.

I'll be sold to Jaguar, of course, and thrown into yet another hell.

But as the seconds pass, I realize that his statement wasn't a threat. It was a reminder.

"You want to learn more? Then follow my lead for now. I need you blissfully ignorant, and I need you to put on a damn good show. Prance around naked if you want, throw your ass in the face of any man to pass by. Give me that time, and I promise you, I will do whatever it takes to keep you alive."

"Alive and not sold," I prod, mistrustful of any way he might play the semantics to his benefit. "Alive and not your captive. Alive and—"

"Alive and with far more freedom than you entered this mess having. Don't pretend that you were living of your own free will before. You were already a prisoner before I took you."

I flinch, blinking my eyes open to find him still glowering at the wall, his head lowered, knuckles white with how hard he has his hands pressed against the stone.

I'm startled by how drastically rage can transform him. Consume.

Though, in a way, it makes sense, reinforcing just how expertly he's lived under his lies. I'm only seeing five years of the rage and hate he's been suppressing all along.

And God, is it terrifying.

"Be a good girl, and you'll have my balls in a vice, little Ada," he adds gruffly. "That's what you wanted from the start, isn't it?"

It is. Only now, I want his literal balls and a real metal vice to crush them with.

Still, I'm not stupid enough to stick my nose up at the only shred of honesty he's offered me. I'll worry about the details and the morality of it later. For now, I'm desperate for some shred of hope.

Something to fight for.

"Fine, Domino," I tell him softly. "I'll be a good girl and play my role. After all, I was born to play pretend, wasn't I?"

His nostrils flare, his expression guarded. "I suppose you were. Go—" He inclines his head to the balcony. "Get cleaned up. Ines will call you for dinner. I suggest you think long and hard about how exactly you plan on being a good girl and don't second-guess that decision. I'll only ever extend my trust to you once. Remember that."

His words haunt me as I lurch from the room on trembling legs, still dripping blood as I go.

CHAPTER ELEVEN

"Dinner will be served on the terrace soon, Miss," Ines calls from the doorway, jarring me awake.

I peel my eyes open with a groan, feeling more exhausted than I did when I finally rested my head on these pillows. I'm in my pretty white room, but this time I remember how I got here—I practically crawled, merely to escape Domino and his blood-stained bathroom.

This room isn't a much better prison, but at least he isn't here. Neither is Alexi, though I'm sure both are still on the property somewhere. Stupidly, I hope that Domino regulated her to her own virtual jail cell on the other end of the estate.

But no.

I can hear her, giggling uncontrollably somewhere beyond this room. Her voice alone isn't what sets every nerve in my body on edge—it's the deep, masculine tone that accompanies it.

Jealously is the last emotion I should feel at a time like this. If anything, I should be relieved that someone has his attention other than me.

Until I hear him speak. "You know I don't play fair," he says, sounding so prideful of that fact, his voice devoid of any of the rage he displayed earlier this morning.

Because it was all an act, of course, him claiming that he needed me to play along with his game. He was lying then, I realize with a sense of dread that guts me.

I was the idiot who fell for it. All along, he's been scheming with Alexi, manipulating me for their own gain. They're in this together.

"Just this once," Alexi taunts in that sexy little purr. "Make an exception for me."

I don't strain to listen to Domino's reply, if he answers her at all. Instead, I climb to my feet, groaning as pain shoots through my skull. Disoriented, I sway, forced to grab the edge of the mattress for balance, and I don't know how much time passes before I can stand without shaking.

Enough time, it seems, for Alexi to get her way, because a series of giggles taunts me next, sounding fainter, from the direction of the terrace.

Ignoring them, I stagger into the closet and grab the first item I can reach, pulling it on without inspecting it in full. Then I return to the mirror and brace myself for what I might find.

Nothing I imagined comes even close to the specter awaiting me from the glass' surface.

She's so pale, her eyes bloodshot, her arms and legs speckled with bruises. My nose is unmarked, at least, though sensitive to the touch.

If Domino wanted to pretend that I was here willingly, he'd have to have a damn good explanation for why I'd submit myself to this kind of abuse. What was that he mocked me with?

You like it rough…

For a second, I reconsider everything. Forget trusting him—I should run. Now. I even start toward the hall with every intention of racing for the front door, his ruse be damned.

But then I hear them, both laughing as though they don't have a care in the world. Domino's voice rings out, unabashedly booming in a cadence that sounds so damn…genuine.

Curiosity alone is what spurs me to turn around and creep past the circular foyer and out onto the terrace.

It's a blindingly bright day, with a beautiful blue sky above and a gentle warmth emanating from a blazing sun. Gone are the storm clouds from earlier. It's a perfect hour to lounge around the fire pit on the terrace's mid-level. Domino claims one of the seats facing me, his head inclined against the back of it.

Alexi sits across from him, practically spilling out of her own chair to face him, her laughter easily reaching across the terrace.

"My round," she taunts. "Think you can beat me at least once?"

Domino flashes a grin that has me stopping short. It's fleeting, but bright enough to transform his entire face into that of a stranger's, relaxing his afternoon away.

Until he sees me.

He sits forward, palming his knees with both hands, his eyes cutting to slits. It's as if he has some internal switch designed to instantly wipe all emotion from his face. Alexi says something to him though I can't make out exactly what it is.

His frown deepens, his jaw clenching as if he remembered his own rules. We're supposed to be here under slightly different roles. He's my rescuer, and I'm his very grateful victim.

It strikes me now how I could send his ruse toppling with very little effort on my part. I could scream. Demand he let me go. Cause a scene.

And he's afraid I'll do just that. I can see the lethality in how he tracks every step I take once I remember how to move again. He's hunting me, desperate for any excuse to lunge and drag me back into that room.

A strange feeling unfurls in my chest, and I don't know how to identify it at first. Not until I finally reach the lower level and draw even with the playful couple.

This feeling? It's power.

"Look who decided to join us," Alexi says, though I notice that most of the playfulness is gone from her voice, leaving it hollow. I sense her eyes trace me up and down, not that I pay her any notice.

My sole focus is Domino. He sizes me up with a cautious glance, trying to decipher just what I'll do next. Do I remember our flimsy excuse for a truce?

I do. And that's the frustrating part. As much as I hate him, I can't deny one awful truth—I *need* him. For now. At least until I can find enough leverage to escape him once and for all.

So, I make myself smile and sway my hips so that I'm sauntering toward him, just as playful as he appeared to be seconds ago.

The way he stiffens gives me immense satisfaction—but it's fleeting. Because playing my role in this instance means I have to touch him, and this moment is so different from the hundreds of other times I've toyed with men I wasn't attracted to.

He's wearing white today, a shirt buttoned as he usually wears it while being here at least—the top two undone. A loose pair of white slacks gives him a casual air that his rigid jawline contradicts. As serious as he looks now, no one could ever mistake this man for anything but a jailer on red alert.

Because of me. I rouse this dark nature in him. I saw it for myself—he wasn't like this with Alexi. Does that bother me?

I can't tell as I push down my revulsion and palm his chest, urging him back into the more relaxed posture he held before.

To my shock, he relents to the pressure, spreading his legs as if sensing my intentions before I even lower myself onto his right knee. His body is stone beneath me—he's wary. I think if it weren't for our audience, he'd shove me to the floor—and make it hurt.

So I draw out the motion, settling back against his chest while I seethe inside. Turning to him, I see his eyes cut to mine and flinch. I want nothing more than to run away. Hide.

But this is what he wanted, isn't it? For me to play pretend.

Well, luckily for him, I've perfected how to do just that. He accused me of being a whore and faking it, but he has no idea how good I can be. How real it can feel to have someone pretend to adore you.

Only to rip it away the second they've gotten what they wanted from you.

It's a feeling reminiscent of what Pia made me feel all those years ago. Like I truly had an ally in this world, someone I could rely on outside of my father's control.

When all the while, she was laughing behind my back.

I'm not laughing now. Forcing my lips into an even wider grin, I place my hand against Domino's cheek, urging him to face me.

"What's so funny?" I ask, and damn. I'm impressed with myself. I sound giddy enough to put Alexi's chirping to shame, and Domino's gaze becomes unreadable in response.

"We were just chatting about old times," Alexi pipes up, and I recognize the note in her voice. That of a bitch who already believes she has her claws sunken into her chosen prey.

The only problem for both of us is that Domino is no one's plaything.

"We'll catch up later," he says to Alexi without taking his eyes off me. I shudder inwardly at the challenge lurking within those haunting green irises—along with a clear warning. "Ada-Maria missed lunch. Could you inform Ines that she can bring her meal out here? I'll make sure she eats every bite."

"Okay."

Alexi doesn't sound too enthusiastic, but the second she disappears from view, I attempt to shift my weight from his lap entirely.

His hand latches onto my knee before I can, effectively riveting me in place.

"You seem cheerful this afternoon," he remarks in a voice like sin. It's a low, husky baritone that anyone who happened to overhear might mistake for warm, considering my position on his lap.

But as his nails graze my flesh in a teasing swipe, I know exactly what he intends—to have me shivering, choking down a hard swallow.

"I hope you slept well, Ada."

"I-I did," I counter, failing to keep my voice level. It shakes, and I know my fear leeches into my carefully constructed mask. So much for fighting him on an even playing field. I can barely keep my composure for longer than a few seconds at a time.

I keep equating his hand on my thigh to the same grip he had around my neck, plunging me beneath the water. If I hadn't hurt myself, would he have kept going?

I can't tell just by looking at him.

He's smug again, the corner of his mouth lifted in a subtle smirk.

I hate him. And that hate makes me petty enough to keep playing with fire.

"I thought of you," I tell him, lowering my mouth near his ear despite the tension his nearness inspires. I even manage to laugh, just once. "My hero. And I slept like a baby."

"Good," he growls in return.

I can't see his expression fully from this angle. All I have to go on is his hand, stroking higher to bridge the gap between my legs. Too high. He's boldly reaching beneath the hemline of my dress, and I can't stop him.

"It couldn't have been a very good dream," he remarks with faux concern. "You're not dripping wet like a cat in heat."

I clamp my thighs together, heedless of his hand between them. He's won. I try to wiggle from his lap again, and he shrugs as if to nonverbally dare me to.

But then I make the mistake of looking over into his eyes. Those smug, confident, incredible fucking eyes.

They make me reckless, and I recall the few times I managed to make those very eyes widen.

With provocation.

"If you're my hero, as they say, Domino… Shouldn't I *always* be dripping wet for you? Ready and willing. My hero."

He grunts, conveying a mixture of irritation and grudging amusement.

"My Ada." He works his other hand into my hair, tugging ruthlessly hard as he goes. "Such a good, happy girl this afternoon. I think I should come up with a reward for you being so cheerful."

My grin falls flat before I can even think to salvage it. Panic sends every coherent thought scrambling.

I want to run.

You can't give in, a part of me warns, even as my muscles twitch with every intention of me lurching to my feet. *You do that now, and he wins.*

And in spite of everything he's done, I can't let him dominate every interaction. Not again. Therefore, risks must be taken. My father called it "the fucking kamikaze" method, where a man puts all of his effort into one harebrained scheme with the hopes that even if it backfires, it takes out at least some of his enemies.

That method got him to the top of Terra Rodea's political scene.

But he didn't have to navigate a man like Domino Valenciaga in this manner. I'm at a loss of how to manipulate him. How to keep him on edge. How to keep up.

All I can do is meet his dare and not flinch. Instead, I lean in, grazing my lips against his chiseled jawline, ignoring the pain lancing through my nose as it's nudged by his.

"A grateful girl should want any reward her hero can give her," I say, letting my voice dip down to a hum that isn't quite as shameless as Alexi's.

I can feel a rumble through his chest as he exhales, even more suspicious than before.

"But when do I get what I really want?" I ask, inclining my head to face him directly.

His wicked smile steals my breath away as he runs his fingers through my hair. "After four days of being a good girl, you'll get what you deserve," he says softly. "In fact, here's your next chance to prove just how good you can be."

I stiffen with alarm as his gaze drifts to something behind me. When I turn, though, I only find Ines approaching from the direction of the house, a silver tray in hand.

She places her bounty on a low table set in the middle of the couches and respectfully nods.

"Thank you," Domino says, dismissing her. Once we're alone again, he palms my waist with both hands, settling me more firmly on his lap. I'm straddling him now. My knees are the only parts of me that have any contact with the couch at all, barely touching down on either side of him.

"Now it's time for you to continue being such a good girl." His voice contains a chilling hint of malice despite his blank expression. Leaning forward, he jostles me against him, and I realize that he picked an item of food from the platter. A piece of strawberry that he cradles between two fingers. "Eat."

My stomach churns. I want more than anything to deny him. On second thought, I want to preserve my pride more. The need for control and the desire for victory go to war within me. It only takes a second for one to win out.

I open my lips and smother any hesitation, allowing him to place the sliver of berry on my tongue. I think I see surprise cross his face for a split-second before his eyes narrow to convey another sentiment entirely. Challenge accepted.

He grabs another morsel of fruit and dangles it just beyond the reach of my mouth. I have to lean forward to take it, biting into the ripe berry dangerously close to his fingertips. At the last second, something makes me swipe my tongue along the pad of one, licking away any remaining juice.

His sly grin falls flat, his chest rumbling again.

The sound does something to me, working with the warm air and the hot sun to make my breathing quicken and my chest tighten. I'm painfully aware of how large he is, and how dangerously close I'm seated near the front of his slacks. The loose fabric conceals any telltale bulge or sign of arousal. I'd have to touch him to be sure.

"You are in a good mood, today," Domino remarks, though he doesn't sound as smug about that as he did just minutes ago. "I wonder just what my Ada-Maria is thinking to feel so damn happy."

I take my time swallowing down my berry. Then I lick my lips deliberately slow, and I don't miss the way his eyes dart down to track the motion.

"I'm thinking of all the ways I can show my hero how grateful I am for what he's done to me."

I've gone too far, failing to disguise the hate in my voice behind fake charm. Rather than dwell over the fact, I relish the wary way he eyes me while letting one of his hands slide from my hip.

"Such a bold girl today, as well." And yet, for the time being anyway, he seems content to grab another offering from the tray and shove it against my mouth.

I eat, and I eat, and I eat, ignoring any discomfort or anxiety building at the back of my mind. This is war, and as such, I have to fight just as dirty as he seems willing to.

"You seem happy today as well," I remark after taking a blueberry from his hand. "I'm sorry if I interrupted your fun and games." I soften my voice, posing my lips in a playful pout.

He scoffs. "Simpering isn't a good look on you, Ada," he scolds. "I like you better when you run that smart fucking mouth."

Challenge accepted.

"How do I know I'm not the game being played?" I demand, raising an eyebrow of my own. Our expressions must mirror each other's now, equally guarded and mistrustful. "You seem to be having so much fun with Alexi. How do I know you're not setting me up?"

"You don't," he replies, snatching a piece of what looks like cheese from the tray next. "Though, believe me, it wouldn't take nearly half as much effort as you seem to think. Eat."

I open my mouth, still mulling over his words. He wouldn't waste the effort to play me, but he seemed unwilling to outright deny that his interactions with Alexi were part of a mind game.

"Don't tell me that you're taking advantage of her, Domino," I murmur after chewing.

It would serve the bitch right. And yet…

I can't be jealous, so that can't possibly be the reasoning behind the pang I feel in my chest. Even during his entire tenure as my father's trusted bodyguard, he never tried so hard with me. He never played "games," or reminisced about the past or lounged so visibly relaxed in my presence. Most notable of all, I never once heard him laugh.

Never like that.

"Don't tell me you're jealous, Ada-Maria," Domino counters. The amount of genuine disgust in his voice warns that he would disapprove of that scenario.

Rather than take the bait, I shrug and dutifully sample the food he's holding before me. "Why would I be? You cared for me enough to bring me here, and protect me from the big bad men who tried to kill me. I'm the fool who would willingly stay here, gladly accepting whatever lies you told me to explain my parents' supposed deaths and everything else going on. Damn. I know you think so little of me, but I must be known for being quite the dumb bimbo for even your accomplices to buy that."

His eyes flash in a subtle warning. "I don't think you should go around pontificating on what those big, bad men might want to do to you, Ada. You'll give yourself nightmares. I suggest you continue to be so damn accommodating and keep your mouth shut."

"Unless I have a cock stuffed in it, right?" I can't resist the taunt, and for whatever reason, it seems to rile him beautifully.

His nostrils flare, and both of his hands return to my hips, gripping tightly to readjust my weight against him.

"Right," he murmurs, his eyes staring dead into my own. "Maybe we should test that theory; what with you being so damn agreeable all of a sudden?"

I swallow hard at the threat, fighting to keep my breathing steady. I can feel his muscle flexing beneath me, his thighs drifting further apart as if to accommodate a growing body part he can't ignore. He's gritting his teeth, a muscle in his jaw lurching.

As foolish as it is to admit, even to myself, I'm not sure what could be getting him hard in this scenario. Our banter? Or the mention of Alexi?

"I would gladly let you utilize my mouth however you see fit," I say, wrenching my gaze down to his mouth, a safer territory than his eyes. Or so I think until he seizes the flesh of his lower lip between his teeth and a growl rumbles through his chest. "If only you didn't have another willing mouth at the ready close by. I'm sure you already got up to plenty of fun and games while I was out. Why let me ruin your fun?"

I'm done with this game. I brace my hand against his chest to pull back and stand. He tightens his grip, easily keeping me locked in place.

"I haven't had fun since the last time your pretty little lips were occupied with me," he warns, and I suck in a breath, suddenly dizzy. The heat in his voice is far too dangerous. As if he means every word. "You would know if you were interrupting anything I didn't intend for you to see."

I flinch. It's a blatant hint that he's been toying with me all this time, with or without Alexi's consent. I don't know what to make of that. Then it strikes me that's exactly what he wants—to confuse me of his motives and leave me constantly second-guessing my own instincts.

I only let myself consider my following actions for a split second. Then I lean forward, deliberately rocking my hips into his. As much as I hate him…

He's all rigid muscle, and I gasp when I feel the firmness of his thighs against my ass. He stiffens, digging his fingers into my waist, only his hands slip, and he's palming my ass instead. I smother any urge to pull away, letting his hands linger, fingers spread apart over both cheeks.

"Don't tell me you've been faking your fun all this time, Domino," I taunt.

He laughs. Then he drives his nails into my flesh—harshly —and I can't smother a cry.

"As it turns out, I am *very* good at faking, Ada," he tells me, nudging my earlobe with his mouth. Then something warmer brushes the lobe with a teasing swipe. His tongue?

I can't let myself get distracted. I just focus on his words and realize what they imply. He's still playing with my head, trying to keep me off balance.

"So am I," I say, palming his cheek so that he's forced to face me again. He's frowning, and a prickle of alarm nips at my spine, warning me to tread carefully. Even if he seems to want information from me—badly enough to agree to a hostile cease-fire—I know better than to push him too far.

So I consider my next course of action the equivalent of a friendly tap.

"I am very good at faking, remember?"

"I remember." His eyes glint with a dangerous gleam. "I've personally watched you 'fake it' many, many, many times."

I cringe at the insinuation—that his claims to have spied on me were all true. And yet, there is one way to use this to my advantage.

"So then you know that even if you do sell me, I'll have no problem faking it then. I'll fake it for whoever can give me a lifeline, no matter how flimsy, and you can lounge around this big, empty house knowing that I'll be comparing them all to you."

It's a boast that riles him like no other. He jolts forward, nearly knocking me backward, if his hands didn't happen to clench against my ass, snatching me to him. Our pelvises collide, my breasts pressed against his collar as though it's a platter.

And I'm the only meal he has any interest in devouring.

CHAPTER TWELVE

I've angered him. His eyes latch onto my mouth, and when he yanks me forward again, I'm sure he'll bite me outright, like a true beast.

He kisses me instead. What my brain processes as a kiss anyway, the act of two mouths meeting for longer than a peck.

But Domino doesn't suck at my mouth sweetly to compel me to silence. He brutalizes. His tongue lashes at mine like a whip, demanding submission. Nothing more, nothing less.

But it shouldn't feel so damn good.

He makes me fight to keep up with him or risk being consumed. I have to meet every prodding jab of his tongue with one of my own. Open my mouth further to let him in. Take him in.

In so many ways, this feels more intimate than even sucking his cock. I can hear him more clearly—feel him in my head. His grunts of pleasure when he nips me with his teeth. His startled hiss when I bite him back.

His heartbeat rages, hammering through my breasts as the scrape of my dress' fragile material irritates my nipples into sharp, stabbing peaks.

He grips me tighter, practically kneading the flesh of my ass until I'm arching my back to escape the pressure. Then leaning into it…

God, he makes me hate myself. My body turns against me, and my brain struggles to keep up. I hate him. Hate him…

And yet, I shiver in anticipation as he slips his fingers beneath the hem of my dress, finding the bare skin of my ass.

And the delicate, sensitive valley in between.

I jump, unable to silence a cry of alarm—one he greedily swallows before letting me withdraw.

My lips sting, my heart racing as I realize how close we are —practically skin on skin. If it weren't for the fabric of his pants…

We'd practically be fucking. A pang shoots through me, joining a pulsing pressure building in between my legs. Gritting my teeth, I ignore it.

"Not entirely a good girl after all," Domino remarks, leaning back, his posture casual once more. To any onlooker, at least. I can feel the tension ripping through him, and I have a terrifying suspicion that I'm not the only one smothering an ache.

Though, as if to counter the mere possibility of him being unable to resist me, he brings his hand to his mouth, taking the pad of his thumb between his lips.

My throat goes dry as I realize where that finger has been.

"One day, you'll beg me to take you there." He says it so casually I'd laugh were he any other man. But his tone lacks the pleading desperation theirs would carry. He's so confident of the inevitable he doesn't even bother to put effort into stating as much.

He'll take me there.

"Ticktock," I manage to croak. "I only have four days to prove how good I can be after all."

His eyes narrow. Sensing his thinning patience, I'll take this as my cue to leave.

When I ease myself off of him, he doesn't react, letting me stand on my own. I'm bold enough to turn toward the house and take a step, though who knows where I'll go once I'm inside. Somewhere far from him to regroup and think. I need to stay focused on my goal—finding a way to get out of this alive. I should be hunting down any information, not humoring him.

Though I can't escape the feeling that anything worth learning wouldn't be kept in the house. He must have another hiding spot somewhere, in a place he thinks I won't reach.

"Wait." His voice rings out when I've barely gone beyond the ring of white couches.

"Yes?" I stop, though I don't dare look back.

"I think it's time we take a swim. Somewhere where we can discuss the duties of a good girl in private."

My heart aches; it's pounding so hard. I have to physically make myself breathe. In and out…

"I don't have a bathing suit," I wheeze in a ragged exhale.

"Good. I don't intend for you to wear one. After all, my good, grateful girl would hide nothing from her hero."

The bastard.

My eyes burn with frustration at how easily he can yank my chain—literally and figuratively. My only consolation is that he hasn't retrieved that despised collar from wherever he's hidden it since my escape attempt.

I want to deny him. I even start to, my lips parting.

Then I recall the tidbit he snuck within the mocking banter —*discuss in private.*

Apparently, he wants to talk to me outside of Alexi's earshot. Recalling this morning, how he ran the shower before making his offer, I have to admit that it's a convincing stunt.

So I'll play one more round of his sick game.

Still, I can't resist a desperate attempt to turn the tables, no matter how small a move it might be. As I spin to face him, I run my hands along my hips, bunching up the material of my dress as I go. Slowly, I wind it up, up, eventually lifting it over my head entirely. Wadding the fabric in a fist, I throw it onto his lap with a final dare. "Lead the way."

His idea of "a swim" occurs in a section of the property I have yet to discover, just past the terrace gardens. There are three levels of the feature in total, each one graded downward to the next until finally the paved path reaches the ground. The amount of landscaping, let alone water, required to maintain such a property astounds me.

Domino lurks just a few steps ahead, his face angled away, shoulders tensing with every step we go. He's paranoid, though he's very good at hiding it. I suspect Alexi isn't the only one he's second-guessing the motives of.

He's wary of me.

"You said once that you owned this land before you started working for my family," I point out.

"I did, and you've been here before." His voice reaches back to me, barely audible above the chirping of insects and bubbling waters of a small fountain we pass. "You don't remember?"

"I think I would remember if Pia owned a place like this," I counter.

If the Ingleciases owned even a fraction of this amount of land—and were able to afford to maintain it like this—I think Pia's life would have been very, very different. She wouldn't have needed to pry her way into my world at all. I could have grown up alone, without her friendship.

The thought stings, and I shy away from it.

"I think we established that your memory can be faulty at times," Domino says, leading me around a bend that coils against the outside of the house. Perched on the hillside above, the structure of it is breathtaking, made of tanned stone and a beautiful array of Spanish architecture mixed with that of an Italian-style villa.

I'm so distracted by the sight, that I almost miss the carefully concealed dig hidden within Domino's reply. Was he referring to my recollections of Pia?

Or of him?

I haven't decided by the time we finally reach our presumed destination.

It's a square-shaped naturalistic pool sunken into the earth, placed close to the hillside. A fake waterfall extends, nearly as tall as the height of the entire terrace itself, compiled of tan stones built into the earth and gently trickling streams of water that enter the pool from three different locations.

Now I'm sure of it—Pia Inglecias definitely didn't possess a property like this a decade ago.

Still, I hold my tongue as Domino approaches the water's edge and strips his shirt before tugging off his slacks. "Get in."

My nakedness feels more heightened here than during the entire walk across the property. This place is shrouded by a row of planted palm trees, not visible from the house itself. I don't spy any hint of the servants who I know lurk throughout the rest of the property.

We feel more alone here than even locked inside his room or in a shower stall.

If I were to scream, I doubt anyone would hear me or even care enough to come running.

"Don't tell me Ada-Maria Pavalos is afraid of a little swim," Domino remarks as he steps down into the water himself. It's so deep that only his head and shoulders are visible once he's waded toward the center. Cold, his eyes meet mine, chilling enough to have me shivering despite the persistent heat. "I know for a fact you're not that shy. Get in."

I choke down my unease and dip my foot beneath the water. It's cool, but refreshing when paired with the full brunt of the sun. I keep going, realizing that a set of broad, stone steps beneath the water's surface help me gradually adjust to the various depths. By the time I join him near the waterfall, I have to kick my legs to keep my head above the water.

He watches me, able to remain standing with his height advantage.

"You seem to know me so well," I rasp, stopping as close to him as I dare.

"I know that you've spent enough time on the yachts of rich men to lose the right to feign caution when it comes to the water," he snipes.

My cheeks flame. I hate how readily he can throw these snippets of my past in my face. Even if I want to deny his insinuations and cruel assertions—I can't. He has five years of information on me stored away, but I have nothing on him. Just snippets and details he may have intentionally left for me to find.

Still, I sense that he's ready for me to start asking some questions of my own. His eyes glitter, electric in contrast to the turquoise water. On second thought, I think he's impatient for me to start asking, like I'm taking longer than he thought.

Maybe because a part of me is rightfully terrified by the potential answers.

"Why lie?" I demand, my voice breaking. "Why pretend that you killed him?"

And then serve his "body" to me in well-cooked pieces.

He inclines an eyebrow as if this wasn't the question he had in mind. Still, he humors me, lifting his shoulder in a shrug that disrupts the water between us. "I will kill him," he clarifies with a finality that leaves me reeling. "But I needed to know if you were just another pawn in his game."

I don't like how his tone shifted over that last statement.

"What do you mean?"

He inclines his head, eyeing me for so long that my legs start to ache from the effort it takes to paddle in place. "I mean, I needed to know if once again Ada was merely playing her role in a larger game on her daddy's say-so."

I blink as his meaning strikes me all at once. "You thought I knew."

It sounds so ridiculous in retrospect. And at the same time, so damn cruel. He wasn't sure if I knew my father's fate, so he decided to test me in the worst way.

Even now, a part of me recognizes that he could still be lying. If he claims to have faked a cooking body, a fake news broadcast would be child's play in comparison.

"I thought your father valued your life more than he apparently does. I was skeptical of how things looked on their face. I'm finding myself warming up to the idea that they are as they look, after all."

More word games and subtle insinuations.

"If you want to turn me against my father, it isn't working," I croak.

Mainly because I'm still in whiplash over the various disruptions in my view of him over the past few days. First, he was on the verge of being indicted. Then he was dead. And now…

"I'm not as stupid as you think I am," I snap, meeting his gaze as he remains rigidly in place while I start to drift, exhausted by the effort of swimming. I drift back to the shallower end, where I can stand with my feet touching the pool's bottom. As a result, there's a good ten feet of distance between us, and I consider climbing from the water altogether. "I know what you're trying to imply."

"What? That your father conspired with your uninspired, politically ambitious, philandering asshole of a boyfriend to use your presumed kidnapping and death to take pressure off of his impending legal battles? Could a man truly be so cruel, Ada-Maria?"

I cringe at the picture he paints, even as I rail against it. "Don't mock me. I know firsthand what my father is capable of."

So does he.

Yet, he raises an eyebrow. "That doesn't sound like a denial."

"He wouldn't," I insist but, for whatever reason, the words sound flat, easily overpowered by the roar of the water surging between the rocks above.

"Come here." He extends his hands behind him, propelling his body toward the largest waterfall, positioned at the very back of the pool. At the same time, the tilt of his chin makes my belly quiver. It conveys a dare he voices in a gruff rasp, "Unless you aren't as confident of your beliefs as you think you are."

I swallow hard before lunging toward him. "I'm *confident* that I don't trust you—"

"You should." When I come within his reach, he grabs my wrist, easily tugging me closer. "I suggest you not take offense to the series of events that have prolonged your life, Ada," he warns, his tone unusually deep.

I stiffen as he drags me toward him, gripping my waist beneath the water. With his strength supporting me, I don't have to fight to stay suspended. Warm, his lips graze my ear, his voice a grated murmur that resonates through flesh and bone, into my belly.

"The possibility that you may be innocent in this scheme of your father's at least, is the only reason why you've kept my attention for as long as you have."

Before I can counter that, he starts to drift, carrying me into an even deeper section of the pool while my thoughts reel. Only our heads are above water now, and I find myself bracing my hands over his shoulders, unnerved by the loss of control. In his grasp, I'm at his mercy. If he decides to pull me under here, I won't be able to fight him.

Satisfied by that very fact, he positions me so that our faces are inches apart, our mouths so close I feel each brush of his lips as he speaks.

"This is the part where I give you permission to run that smart ass mouth of yours," he murmurs.

It's the best chance I've had to question him. So I'll take it.

"Tell me what you want? Who is Jaguar? Why were you fucking Alexi? Why is she even here? How——"

"So greedy," he scolds, flexing his hands against my waist in punishment. Beneath the water, his heat is neutralized by the colder temperature, meaning that I'm forced to contend with the texture of his touch in a way I haven't before. He's strong, every finger resonating a subtle pressure that warns he could easily hurt me if the mood strikes him.

And it already has more than once.

His eyes are unreadable, shrouded by heavy lids that cast shadows over those imperceptible green irises. I can't tell if he's annoyed by my barrage of questions or amused.

"One at a time like the good girl you've been so eager to be."

His tone makes his meaning clear—choose wisely. Piss him off or push too far, and he'll stop.

I lick my lips only to realize that his eyes drift down to track the movement of my tongue from one end of my mouth to the other. His throat lurches, betraying a hard swallow, and I nearly lose track of what it is I'm supposed to be doing.

Right. Learning whatever he's willing to give.

"Tell me about Jaguar."

"*Julian*," he corrects, putting a harsh emphasis on the name. "Tell me something, have you ever heard of Carlos Domingas?"

I frown, recalling the many acquaintances my father had circling around his orbit at any given time. There are too many to keep track of, their names a blur.

"No—"

"You should have," Domino cautions in a way that recalls a disapproving teacher during a complex lecture. "Though I wouldn't be surprised if you haven't. Carlos Domingas was a man your papa knew very well indeed. They were partners, long before Don Roy slipped across the border and became the polished, savvy politician he presents to the world."

I'm curious despite myself. He could be lying, but I don't have the privilege of ignoring him. To his credit, I don't know enough about my father's past to challenge anything he might assert. It was a time in his life he rarely spoke about, not even among family. In fact, he only ever referenced himself as a boy when boasting about his scrappy instincts and cunning that led him to crawl from poverty to where he is today.

My father, the ultimate survivor, fashioning himself as the city's savior.

"Carlos Domingas was a tough son of a bitch. He ran a whole series of enterprises that your daddy would swear now never to have been a part of. That doesn't erase the fact that when Don Roy first entered Terra Rodea all those years ago, he did it hand in hand with Carlos Domingas and the full backing of his cartel."

It's a blunter retelling of the same rumors that have plagued my father's entire career from its inception. That he was a puppet for drug trafficking and used his cozy position with those in power to force the authorities to look the other way or outright ignore corruption.

He's always denied as much, publicly, anyway.

If I had to be honest with myself, the man whispered about in those rumors sounded closer to who I knew my father to be than the way he portrayed himself during his campaign speeches.

"When Roy got too big for his britches, he tried to turn on Carlos Domingas, arranging a hit on him. It was clever, of course, and he covered his tracks. But Carlos Domingas was a man who thrived on revenge. Before Roy ever got the thought in his head of betraying him, Domingas already had ten plots of retaliation set in motion."

"You?" I ask, hazarding a guess.

He grunts out a sound that might pass for a laugh were he anyone else. "In addition to a wealth of cutthroat allies and 'associates,' Carlos Domingas had two sons that he started training to replace him before they were even out of diapers."

His tone prompts me to take another guess.

"Jaguar?" I ask.

He nods. "Julian and a younger brother named Juan. Under the alias, Jaguar, Julian has been amassing his own realm of influence over the ashes of what his father left behind."

"And his brother? What about him?"

His eyes cut away from me, darker than ever. "Dead. Jaguar runs his little kingdom alone."

"But what about you?" I recall a fragment of their conversation I overheard. "He called you little brother—"

"A sick attempt at a joke on his part," Domino says, swatting away the insinuation. "He meant nothing by it."

"So why me?"

He smiles, but there's no warmth in it. With his teeth bared, the expression resembles a snarl. "You, Ada-Maria, are here only by the grace of God. That 'car crash' hit on your father was never intended to kill him, merely distract. It seems, however, that even Roy Pavalos can't walk away from such serious trauma without a scratch. When it seemed like he might die after all, Jaguar had no use for you."

It sounds so cold to hear him state it so bluntly, reducing my worth to my mere designation as the daughter of Roy Pavalos.

"He was tempted, you see, to let Tristan Lucas put his little plan in action to hog the glory of your apparent abduction and claim the vacuum left by the impending death of Roy Pavalos. He would have been a very useful pawn to have under Julian's thumb. However, I managed to convince him to sever such sloppy loose ends."

His tone deepens, devoid of all emotion. It's how he sounded while conversing with my father, accepting any and every task he would hand down. I used to marvel at how one man could seem so detached from the world. From emotions. From everything.

And yet, I hoarded over every brief glimpse I managed to catch of the real creature lurking beneath that mask. Perhaps I fantasized so much about that hypothetical Domino that I lost sight of the stark reality of who he was. Who he's always been.

A soldier following orders, with no moral compass of his own.

"He's let me keep you merely to placate me for the time being," Domino adds, bringing his mouth near my ear again.

We're still floating through the water, my thighs resting against his hips, his hands still on my waist to hold me steady. I think this is the longest we've been so close.

Apart from during sex.

"Why?" I ask him hoarsely.

His brows furrow as he returns his gaze to mine. "Your father's condition, though critical, is rapidly improving," he says, ignoring that I've spoken. "Which means that your usefulness to Jaguar has just skyrocketed. He's let me keep you for now because I'm shouldering the logistics of keeping you hidden from the manhunt searching for you, and he doesn't have to take the risk. Yet. But trust me, Ada, he'll come for you, and he won't be your knight in shining armor."

"And you are?"

He frowns at the slight, but seems to let it slide without comment. Instead, he shifts so that my back is to the outcroppings of rock. I can feel stray droplets of moisture speckle me from above, and the gentle hum of the water is even louder here.

"I have my own uses for you," he admits.

Suddenly, he lifts me from the water, and I scramble for purchase, gripping a firm surface in return. With a start, I realize that he's set me down on a rocky ledge while remaining in the water, in between my legs.

Through his lashes, his eyes seem even more intense than usual. He's like some fucked up, masculine version of a merman, his damp hair clinging to his shoulders, body bare.

Without warning, he grabs my chin, balancing it against the palm of his hand.

When seconds tick by without him expounding on his statement, I once again get the feeling that he's waiting for me to prod him for more. In this instance, he wants me to.

"What do you want?"

A dangerous smirk flits across his lips before a sterner expression replaces it. He's scrutinizing me carefully, sizing me up by the time he's done. And yet he's not nice enough to voice his impression of me, out loud.

I have to guess from the way his fingers flex against my skin, startlingly soft... Until his nails tease my flesh to give me a taste of the pain he's capable of inflicting.

"You once claimed that everyone wants to use you to get to your father. Well, you've gotten your wish. I want *you*—fuck Roy Pavalos. But unfortunately, Ada-Maria, I won't just tell you why. I want you to guess."

My eyes sting, and the moisture falling from them catches me off guard. Tears. As they lash down my cheeks, I realize why they've sprung forth now.

It's so very cruel, the way he's toying with me. Days ago, I would have died to hear those very words. I'd have done anything.

But now I know that beneath them lurks a million secrets and lies. They mean nothing on their face.

I want *you.*

I wish he'd claim to use me against my father instead.

"You hate him," I point out, craving more than anything that I had the strength to shove him aside and swim away. I need to get away—because I can't hide it. Not my pain or the grim reality that these tears are real and I'm not faking anymore. "Everything you've done to me has been retaliation against him. For Pia. For whatever you think he did—"

"This was never just about him," Domino interjects, his tone cutting. "I warned you of that fact once. I suggest you listen to me, and that you never underestimate Julian."

His eyes blaze. He means every word, displaying a hostility that I don't think I've ever seen him exhibit, not even toward me.

"What about Alexi? How is she involved in all of this?"

Some of the bitterness leaves his gaze, and I hate that I react to that, my chest tightening. "She is a pawn of Julian's, nothing more. I don't feel strongly about her either way," he adds, conveying a hint of mercy toward her that he's never shown me. "But she works for him. Do not forget that, and I would advise against thinking of her as an ally."

I let the jab pass unchallenged, fixated on the way he said that—*she works for him.* In his cold baritone, he might as well have said—*she belongs to him.*

"How did she meet him? How did you meet her?"

He strokes the length of my jawline as he withdraws his hand from my chin, returning it to my unclaimed thigh. "I'll let you ask her those questions, if you're truly that curious."

I hiss in exasperation. "First, you warn me not to talk to her. Then you dare me to—"

"I don't want you to forget…" His voice softens, and I have to strain to hear him. "I'm the only one you can trust."

I recoil as far as I dare without risking my balance, crossing my arms over my exposed breasts. "My father said that," I reply.

He laughs, but it's a sharp, vengeful sound. "I think we both know for a fact that I am not your daddy, Ada-Maria. At least not in that context."

My breath catches, my cheeks flaming. It's suddenly hard to suck in enough air to breathe.

"I… You… You were fucking Alexi," I say, latching onto the next topic demanding an explanation. "I saw the pictures."

Pictures that he alluded to leaving for me to find in the first place.

His smile returns in full, ripening as his eyes take on a playful, wicked gleam. "You know better than anyone, Ada-Maria. A picture is worth a thousand words. Fake, useless words meant to spin a narrative. You yourself have starred in dozens of photos that might portray a reality that differed from the truth. Videos as well."

I hate how easily he wields my own past against me. The worst part is that I can't accuse him of lying. If anyone would know, he would. He was right when he claimed my father would want confirmation that I followed his orders. And, like a good dog, he gladly followed after me, gathering evidence as he went.

"Tell me, Ada, were your simpering smiles and moans genuine then?"

I flinch. He knows precisely where to prod to slip beneath my defenses. I can't resist wondering if anything else he hinted at was true. Like that my father was indifferent to my impending kidnapping all along…

And my death.

No. He was lying, of course. Besides, I have to stay focused. Meeting his gaze, I look past my own fear and try to find a weakness of his to exploit.

"Whatever your relationship with Alexi is, you were with her," I point out. "And yet, you don't seem to have a problem with her 'belonging' to Jaguar now. But…"

His nostrils flare, conveying a warning I fail to heed.

"You don't seem too willing to share me with him. Why is that?"

He spreads his fingers out along my inner thighs, and I suck in a breath, grappling for a better grip on the rock beneath me.

"Because I never wanted Alexi." He lowers his head, leaning forward so that his mouth comes dangerously close to my breasts, his gaze fixated below my waist.

I gasp as he nudges my legs apart, easily claiming the space between them.

"I never claimed Alexi. I never spent five fucking years wondering what she tasted like. I never cultivated a kill list of all the men she casually fucked—" His nails dig in as he spreads my legs further, fully opening me to him. The heat of his breath lashes me in searing waves, and my eyelids flutter, my brain paralyzed by the sensation. He's growling, real anger seeping into every single syllable. "I never wanted her so badly I could get hard at just the sight of her smile. I'll let you parse over those words, Ada-Maria. I'll let you decide what that means."

He lunges downward, and I barely manage to throw my hands in between us, feeling his mouth brush my trembling fingers.

"W-Wait," I croak.

Not stop.

He looks up, eyeing me through a fringe of black hair, his eyes so vibrant they practically glow.

"I know you're just toying with me," I rasp, but it should be the least of my concerns at the moment, his approval. His lust.

Besides, my sloppy phrasing was a pathetic way of avoiding what I really mean—*I know you're lying to me.*

"Good," he says, his voice gruff. "I want you to think of that while I have my tongue buried inside of you. I want you to tell yourself that over, and over until it hurts, Ada. That pouty face you make when you doubt me… It's sexy as hell."

CHAPTER THIRTEEN

I can't stop him this time. My hands are easily batted aside, and I wind up grasping for the nearest source of stability I can find as his heat sears the flesh between my legs. It's so soft, whatever it is, like I'm grasping at silk—his hair, I realize.

It's my turn to rake my nails over his skull and pull as he does exactly what he warned he would.

He buries his tongue inside of me.

In this instance, I have no frame of reference to compare him to. As it turns out, most of the men I've slept with were only interested in their own pleasure, never mine. I was just a smiling, warm sex doll. The closest anyone came to attempting to get me off manually was Tristan, and only with his fingers, sloppily with no real effort put into the act.

But Domino…

Eat is such a dangerous word—so vulgar to describe simply putting your mouth on someone. When a woman sucks a cock, it's not described so viciously.

But the feeling assaulting me now can only be described by terms that should never apply to something like sex. Devoured. Swallowed. Choked down. Worshiped...

He turns my body into his altar, and then he douses me in sin. After sin. After sin.

I scream, writhing as his lips press against my inner flesh, while his fingers come to spread me open. Ruthlessly expose every inch and fold. Then his tongue lashes, hot and violent, irritating every single nerve to a painful degree.

His teeth graze me next, and I jerk, trying to push his head again. Then gripping him for dear life as my eyes roll back.

It would be one thing, if he could abuse me in this way, and I'd have to endure it. Suffer through each slow, savoring lick. Keep my senses. Hate him and hate him.

He turns my body inside out instead. Every bit of twitching muscle and heated flesh becomes my enemy, rebelling against the faint sliver of my brain fighting for control.

I whimper, realizing it's too late to shut him out. His tongue easily slips inside of me, molten hot. My body welcomes him, each drop of moisture flooding like gasoline toward the lips and tongue working in tandem like a match and tinder.

I'm on fire. Too hot. Burning alive. Melting. Ashes.

Then, just when my stomach stops flipping, and I can breathe again, he keeps going…

Shame is a concept that feels harder to grasp with every brutal, gut-wrenching orgasm he wrings from me. My spine is his toy, my limbs jelly, my voice so hoarse and broken I can't speak.

Hurting him is the only language I have left to communicate with him. Raking nails and tugging fingers.

But he's impervious, no matter how hard on his scalp I pull.

"…faking." I feel his voice vibrate through me; it's so guttural, overpowering every other sound to ripple through my skull. "So good at faking. My Ada. *Keep* faking."

He's taunting me, and I don't even have the sense of mind to counter him.

My moans are shameless, reduced to whispered gasps as my voice breaks. I see stars by the time I start to believe he'll finally take mercy on me. He's stopped, his head resting heavily on my thighs, his pants basting the drenched skin between my legs.

"I imagined roses," he rasps, tilting his head so that his eyes find me.

I'm too sensitive. Too raw. With one look, a pulse shoots down my spine, and I flinch; it's damn near painful. One look, and it's like he's touching me all over again.

"Or bubblegum, or some shit," he adds, his eyes narrowing. Slowly, he trails his tongue across his wet lips, tasting whatever moisture is there. The flavor must anger him. Infuriate. He glowers at me, through damp strands of black hair that frame his face like scorch marks. My devil, enraged by my taste. "How is it possible that you taste better than that?" he demands.

"Please," I croak as he lowers his gaze, crouching between my legs again.

I'm panting, my back on fire, ass scraped raw by the stone beneath me. "Please... Enough."

As if he would ever show me mercy.

Ruthlessly, his mouth engulfs me again. Torments me again.

The pleasure is so sharp and intense it borders on painful. It *is* pain, every hungry, groping touch from him. Every slow, relishing lick.

Eating is the only word that comes close to describing what it feels like. With nibbling, greedy tastes, he devours me whole.

I lose track of time and space. I just know that when the pressure finally relents, I'm leaning against a sturdy surface, softer than stone, but just as impenetrable.

"I've got you," he says in a voice so rough my toes curl. "I've got you, Ada... Always, I've got you."

Something in his tone reaches through my dazed, dizzying thoughts to some part of me beneath that stirs in alarm. It's hard to remember why I should be. Why I shouldn't relent to the grip of the man holding me against his chest, cradling my head against his shoulder, as he propels us both through the water. Why I should hate…

It's like being amid the throes of the wildest, reckless, dangerous high. The rules of reality start to blend and blur, and my giddy brain tells me that anything is possible. Even the prospect of Domino Valenciaga craving me in a way that roughens his voice like I've never heard it.

But somewhere in the process of him lifting me from the water and carrying me across the property toward the terrace, my common sense starts to return. I wake up.

With the house looming above, there's no denying who I am or the identity of the man holding me in his arms. I stiffen, scrambling to regain control of my limbs.

"L-Let me go," I demand.

Either he doesn't hear me, or he doesn't care, swiftly mounting the bottom level of the terrace even as my palm lands harmlessly against his chest. I can't see his face fully from this angle. Just a curtain of dark hair and the edge of his jaw, clenched so tightly it's a firm, solid line.

He's facing straight ahead, as though I don't exist, even as he adjusts his grip on my body to keep me contained.

We must have been in the pool for hours. The sun is lower over the horizon, marking the hottest part of the late afternoon, not long before sundown. Bathed in the golden glow, the house looks majestic.

And more inescapable than ever, my beautiful paradise of a prison. Two figures lurk on the topmost part of the terrace, watching our approach.

One is short and diminutive in stature. Ines.

The other is tall and lithe, her blond hair swaying in a light breeze as she leans over the railing.

"Boo! No fair," Alexi calls. "If you were going for a swim, I would have come! We could have played chicken."

I can sense her barely concealed innuendo from here, even without having to see the simpering smile on her face.

Then I realize, that to know we went swimming, she can tell that Domino and I are dripping wet, our hair plastered to our heads. A quick glance down reveals that he donned his slacks at least before heading here.

But I'm still naked. Still raw and overly sensitive, too exhausted to even stand on my own, let alone cover myself.

The knowledge of people watching has me shrinking against him, forced to submit to the width of his arms to cover any exposed parts of me.

And the bastard is enjoying this. He has enough tact not to laugh outright, but I can feel the subtle tremors ripple through his chest. He loves having me unnerved, left with no choice but to rely on him.

A fact that I should always keep at the back of my mind.

I stay alert as he follows the gradual incline of the terrace, eventually winding his way to the top where Alexi and Ines wait, the latter poised for instruction.

"We'll have dinner in the dining room," he says to the maid who dutifully scurries off. Then, Domino inclines his head toward Alexi. "We'll change and meet you there."

I can't look at her directly. Not when my face is on fire, every insecurity I physically possess screaming out in the open for her enjoyment. I'm sure she can see the marks and bruises on my body in stark detail. The slight trembling in my legs.

The wetness leaving Domino's lips glistening.

I'm sure she can connect the dots—but that's not what has me on edge. It's the fear that in her eyes, I'll find a conspiratorial gleam that warns she's not the least bit surprised to see me like this, with him.

Because, every step of the way, she's been in on his plan from the very beginning.

"Can't wait," she says finally, in a flat tone that doesn't reveal her impression of the situation either way.

As Domino heads inside, crossing the threshold of the circular foyer, I can't stop myself from looking back.

She's watching us, one hand casually braced on the railing behind her, her head tilted so that the sunlight hits her from the best possible angle. She's so effortlessly pretty that it hurts, her eyes the same big, endless blue that I remember, her face perfection, perky tits on full display by her lowcut top.

Her smile is cheerful, stretching eagerly across her face.

But in her gaze lurks open suspicion and a quiet hostility that she doesn't bother to disguise. Domino isn't the source of her annoyance, either.

Just me.

As Domino crosses the foyer, she disappears from my line of sight, and I find myself being carried into his room seconds later.

He sets me on the edge of the mattress and strolls for the closet, tugging his slacks down as he goes.

There is a shameless pride in how he stands utterly naked and scans the items hanging from the rails. At first, I assume that he's putting so much scrutiny into picking an outfit for himself. One that will impress a certain blond, perhaps?

Then he fingers the hem of a black skirt, and I realize what he's doing. He's picking out an outfit for me.

I'd forgotten that sometime during the chaos of Jaguar's arrival, he had women's clothing brought here. He scans them all with a familiarity that makes my breath quicken. Like he already has the exact white A-line style dress in mind for me to wear. It's just a matter of finding it.

When he finally approaches, chosen dress in hand, he eyes me with a ruthless sweep of his gaze.

"I'll need to wash you."

I shiver, my head swimming. It's unnerving how he can shift from emotionless to bristling with intensity on a dime.

"I can wash myself." I try to stand, and I barely flex my feet against the floor when I'm assaulted by a million different, conflicting sensations. My various scrapes and injuries are on fire, each one throbbing at full force. Between my legs feels sore, rubbed raw. Even the slightly cooler air inside feels like stabbing knives against that sensitive skin. Forget washing myself; I don't even know if I'm brave enough to risk standing up.

"So damn stubborn." Domino hauls me to my feet by my wrist, making the decision for me.

I'm biting my lip so hard I taste blood as he makes me follow him into the bathroom and lean against the counter. He retrieves a clean cloth from somewhere, wets it beneath the faucet, and then wipes me with a rigorous, clinical focus.

The same way my father maintained his luxury vehicles. It was one of the few tasks he preferred to do himself, waxing them to perfection, ensuring they made the best possible impact.

I'm as much a possession to him as those cars were to my father. I can see the same cold focus in his eyes as he drags the cloth over my belly and between my legs. He's making a note of every scrape and scratch. Every time I flinch and jump when he grazes a barely healed injury.

He's making a mental map of every inch of me.

A man who planned on selling you wouldn't be this obsessive, a part of me warns. I ignore it.

His motives aside, I try to reassemble my logical thought process as I come down from that sexual high. The things he said come rushing back to me, mainly about Jaguar and Alexi.

"Why was she after Tristan?" Is he implying that she was doing so on Jaguar's say-so?

She works for him, he said.

"Why is she here now? What do you—"

He presses a finger to my lips, sealing them with just enough pressure to cut me off.

"You'll get your answers," he says, dropping his rag into the sink. He retreats into the room and returns with the dress bunched in both hands. He motions for me to raise my arms, and when I do, he dresses me, tugging the material down to fall over my hips.

With an appreciative glance, he surveys his work in the mirror. Hunched behind me, he can't disguise the way his eyes dip over the V-shaped neckline. "I knew this one would suit you," he remarks in a voice so subdued I almost miss what he says.

He knew…

I inspect myself, noting that the white dress—like pretty much everything he's had me wear since my arrival—is far beyond the usual norm I'd stick to. It's too bold, and at the same time, too minimal. The demur shade of white makes my eyes look even larger than they are.

In comparison to his bulk, I'm as delicate as a porcelain doll.

A contrast that I think he enjoys.

"Come." He crosses the balcony, reenters the closet, and grabs a shirt and dry slacks, pulling them on with little fanfare. Then he leads the way into the dining room, where Alexi lounges shamelessly against the back of the chair placed at the table's head.

At the sight of Domino, her mouth quirks into a sly smirk as she arches her back so high her nipples threaten to pop out from the neckline of her top. "I'm *starving*," she purrs. "I'm just about ready to stick anything I can get ahold of into my mouth."

The bitch.

She looks past me, her eyes tracking Domino as he claims a seat beside her. His hand latches onto my wrist, forcing me to take the one next to him.

"It's about time we got to catch up, Adie," Alexi says, flicking her attention to me. "Gosh, how long has it been?"

Not long enough, in a sense. For so long, Alexi has so doggedly pursued any man I've had any hint of interest in.

Am I surprised that she managed to dig her claws into Domino?

No. I'm more alarmed by the fact that she succeeded.

She's mastered his talent for poker faces, it seems, her blue eyes unreadable as I meet her gaze. She sits forward, letting her breasts press against the table while she curls a bit of blond hair around her finger.

"Little Adie, all grown up. It's so weird, you know I almost didn't recognize you when I came back."

Two years ago, Alexi Rojas returned from obscurity to make my life hell any way she could. But before then, we were as close as sisters. Not to the same extent Pia and I were, but close enough.

I used to know all of her secrets, and she knew mine. Like the bad little habits we both indulged in, and one she taught me to perfect.

You should keep a toothbrush in your purse, she told me once, as we huddled in the bathroom of a classroom building on the campus of our boarding school. *You can stick it down your throat, and it helps make everything easier. I bet we'll both lose ten pounds by next month, and then no one will dare make fun of you the next time we wear bikinis.*

I thought that was so kind of her. Sweet, actually. It's funny how, despite the world in which I grew up, I could still be so goddamn naïve. To me, back then anyway, Pia and Alexi were the best friends any girl could ever ask for.

I was sure we'd be close forever.

"You look the same," I tell her. "I guess some people keep their baby fat forever. It looks cute on you, though."

Her smile falls flat, and I'm pathetic enough to take a grim sense of satisfaction in that. It's so surreal to see her head, uninjured, her skin unblemished, giggling with Domino like they're old friends. Even now, she keeps herself angled toward him, cleavage on display. It's as if she's become so accustomed to seeking out male attention, she's compelled to do so, even when the male in question seems to have no interest in looking her way.

He's fixated on the windows instead, eyeing the rapidly darkening sky.

"I'm going to check on our meal." He rises to his feet and heads for the hallway. When I start to follow him out of habit, I swear I see him jerk his chin in a silent command. *Stay.* "I'll be back in a moment."

Confused, I stare after him as my heart pounds unsteadily. Given that—in my entire time here—he's preferred to summon servants who appear on a dime, rather than fetch our meals himself, I'm on edge. I'm flashed back to the night he had what he claimed to be my father served on a silver dish. Does he have a similar meal in mind for Alexi's benefit?

Or… I realize as I turn my focus back to the woman in question, he left purposefully. So that we could "catch up" in private.

And what a lackluster reunion it's shaping up to be. Without her required dose of testosterone nearby, Alexi slumps back in her seat, her eyes openly displaying disinterest. Sighing, she inspects a manicured hand, watching the light glint off her pink nails.

It's a convincing show—because that's exactly what I sense it really is. An act.

As the seconds tick by, she grows visibly impatient, waiting for me to make the first move.

Because she's unsure of what I know, a part of me suspects. As much as she seems to hate me, she doesn't want to say the wrong thing. Some sick, twisted corner of my brain gets immense pleasure out of watching her squirm.

But something tells me that Domino won't give us long to reconnect. Is this impromptu opportunity for an interrogation done for her benefit? Or mine.

"So," I say, flattening my hands against the table's glass surface. "How long have you been fucking him?"

Alexi's smile returns in full as her eyes narrow. "You know, I spent a long time trying to imagine how this would feel. To see the high and mighty Ada-Maria Pavalos sniveling in fear for once, cowering in the shadow of a plot she has no damn clue of. I thought I'd feel bad for you. Pity, maybe? In all honesty, I'm enjoying every minute of it. Humility looks good on you, Ada. You should try to embody it more often."

I flinch, and I almost forget Domino's warning from the pool. *She works for him.* And, their apparent relationship aside, it's evident from the lengths he's gone to conceal our conversations that he doesn't trust her.

I have to tread carefully.

Hopefully, I can do so while knocking her down a peg or two.

"Why don't you give me some pointers on humility?" I say. "In between fucking Tristan and Domino, I'm surprised you had room for anyone else."

Her brows furrow for a split second before she disguises the expression behind another forced smile. Still, I know that I confused her. How?

"How has Dom been?" she asks in that husky purr, leaning back against her chair. "Poor man. To have spent so much time under the thumb of the mighty Pavalos family. I bet it was like being in prison. Who knows how much sexual frustration he's built up over those long, hard years? No wonder you look like you've been dragged to hell and back. I think I would have trouble keeping up with that kind of virility, and I've heard that you're the sort of girl who doesn't like to break a sweat."

"Haven't you heard," I croak, desperate to appear unrattled. "I like it rough."

She purses her lips, crossing her arms over her chest. "You know, I never took you for the type to wind up in a situation like this," she says, but I know a taunt when I hear one. "Alone in a big-ass manor with your father's bodyguard and no connection to the outside world. I would have thought that someone who brands herself as a socialite would be a little concerned about what might be happening in Terra Rodea."

I sit straighter, trying to disguise as much of my interest as I can. She's hinting at something, dancing around it. But what?

I'm tempted to ask her outright and drop the caution. Damn Domino and his mind games, I need answers. The only thing holding me back is the knowledge that Alexi would never give me something I wanted. I'd have to trick her into revealing it.

"Why should I care about the big bad world?" I ask with a shrug. "I'm safe here with Domino. If there's something I need to know, he'll tell me."

She smirks, an eyebrow raised. "You really are that fucking gullible."

I get the sense that statement slipped out unbidden, though she does her best to cover the break in composure with a forced laugh.

"I think I'd feel a bit differently. Then again, I always was a bit less self-centered than you."

It's my turn to smirk. "Oh? I agree. You've been so selfless you've been fucking anyone who so much as looks at me. Like Tristan."

She scoffs. "Oh, come off it, Ada. Like you actually gave a damn about Two-second Tristan. For what it's worth, I couldn't stand him. Not only was he bad in the sack, but he had horrible taste in women. I had to practically drool, or he'd lose interest. No wonder he liked you so much. I'll let you in on a little secret, Adie—" She leans across the table, and the breeze carries the scent of her cheap perfume to my nose. "He didn't even tell me he had a girlfriend when he started fucking me—though I already knew, of course. When I finally asked about you, do you know what he said? That he was humoring you out of respect for your powerful daddy. Fancy that."

My brain goes blank. I don't know how to process her nasty digs all at once. Instead, I try to ignore them, looking past the hateful rhetoric to the truth lurking beneath.

"If you didn't like him so much, why fuck him at all? At least I actually had some interest in him." I nearly choke on the lie, not that Alexi seems to notice it.

She's practically lunging across the table, blue eyes blazing. "Why? Don't be such a dumb cunt, Ada. You know. I'm sure Domino told you all about his little scheme. To have me get close to Tristan and suss out all of his bad-boy plots. I know you've made a name for yourself based on being a dumb, blond bitch, but Jesus Christ, you can't even drop the act here?"

"D-Domino had you get close to Tristan?" I croak.

Her raised eyebrow quirks even higher. "He didn't tell you." A shadow falls over her expression as her beautiful features rearrange into a blank mask. She sits back, putting space between us that feels less like a retreat and more like she's hiding something. Or she said too much. "Maybe Domino hasn't been quite as talkative as I thought; what in between all those hot and heavy rounds of screwing."

I don't miss the note of jealousy in her voice then, but I'm too distracted to pounce on it like I should.

Domino manipulated Alexi into sleeping with Tristan. Though, of course, he did. It makes so much sense it should have been evident from the start. He took those pictures of them. He had Tristan's home outfitted with a camera to make secret recordings. He even threw as much in my face, leaving me to put the pieces together on my own.

And yet, it somehow feels ten times more violating to hear it straight from the horse's mouth. Not only was Alexi in on his scheme, toying with Tristan for a reason beyond just getting back at me. She was doing it for Domino.

And he trusted her enough to have her enact his scheming for him.

Suddenly, I don't want to play this game anymore. I don't want to know what else I've been so fucking oblivious to. More and more, it's starting to feel like, once again, I'm the butt of a joke everyone else is in on but me. I'm the pawn being manipulated across the gameboard.

Alexi alluded to the chaos unfolding in Terra Rodea. With my mother dead and my father in the hospital, I can only imagine. What the hell has Domino unleashed?

And what does he really have in mind for me?

I start to push back from the table, too overwhelmed to stay on task. I've barely moved when I sense a presence approach me from behind, bringing with them a scent of cooked meat.

"Dinner will be more informal tonight," Domino explains. His muscular arms reach past me, placing a platter of what looks like meat and vegetable skewers on the center of the table. Ines appears at the other end and sets down a dish of rice and a platter of fruit.

"Can you please bring us some wine," Domino tells her before reclaiming his seat.

Within the blink of an eye, Alexi is back to her smirking, overly extended self. Boldly, she reaches out, placing her hand on Domino's shoulder.

"You didn't have to go through so much trouble," she chirps, but her gaze is on me, narrowed and searching. "I didn't even know Ada loved this kind of food."

Domino turns to me, and I stiffen, unprepared for the intensity I find reflected in his gaze. He cradles my chin against his hand, stroking along my jaw. "She's surprisingly adventurous," he murmurs. "So willing to try different things."

I grit my teeth so hard my jaw cracks. I hate not knowing. I can't tell if they're both allied conspiratorially, playing mind games at my expense.

But this time, I don't suppress the urge to run. I wrench out of Domino's grasp and push back from the table.

"I'm not hungry—"

"You will eat." He somehow manages to sound more charming than threatening. Perhaps it's the grin he flashes that robs the bite from his words. Or the fact that his hand slides against my lower back, unseen from Alexi's position. "We wouldn't want to offend our guest?"

He grabs a skewer of something that looks like seasoned chicken and bites off the top most chunk. Then he hands it to me.

I feel Alexi's gaze on me, itching like a nasty rash. Domino, however, forces eye contact, and I can see the dare written clearly across those green irises. *Eat. Or so help me God, I will shove this stick down your goddamn throat.*

I grab it and take a bite, chewing without tasting. As I swallow, Domino sits back while Ines appears with the bottle of wine. She dutifully pours three glasses, and Domino grabs the one nearest him.

"A toast," he says, lifting his glass to the air. "To old friends."

"And to new ones," Alexi chimes in, taking a drink of her own.

I claim the final serving and bring it to my lips without waiting for him to solidify the toast.

Chuckling, he follows my lead, but I keep going long after he and Alexi set their glasses down again. Until I've drained every last drop.

"You should eat first, Ada-Maria." Domino's tone is swift and cutting. "I wouldn't recommend drinking on an empty stomach."

"You know what I wouldn't recommend?" I toss back.

God, his expression transforms so quickly it's terrifying. He's a beast, teeth bared and ready to bite. I know I'm going too far—every ounce of common sense in my body is warning me to stop. Play along. Trust his promise, even though he's lied, and abused, and brutalized.

By the time I reconsider provoking him now, it's already too late.

"I wouldn't recommend fucking a man who fucks the trailer trash—" Looking Alexi dead in the eye, I add, "Twice."

Then I scramble to my feet, knocking over my chair in my haste to move.

But I'm nowhere near quick enough.

Domino snatches my wrist. "I suggest you sit down, Ada, and return to our meal." He's audibly angry now, unable to carry on his playful ruse.

Good.

I'm done being his little toy.

"I *suggest* you don't kidnap women from the family you work for. That you don't claim to have killed their father or orchestrated an attack that caused the death of their boyfriend." I rip my hand away, but—to my shock and growing alarm—he lets me. "I would also suggest that you don't fuck the town whore, Domino. And maybe next time? Try not to sell me, either."

I run, and surprisingly no one chases after me or throws me down. I make it all the way into the white room, slamming the door in my wake. Then I lock it. Heart pounding, I search for the heaviest thing I can find—a white dresser against the wall near the closet entrance—and I throw my weight against it, pushing it before the door as a makeshift barricade.

I have no delusions that it will hold him. For good measure. I strip the bed of blankets and drag the mattress to the door as well, propping it upright against the dresser for added reinforcement.

Then, like a coward, I race into the closet, close the door and wedge myself behind the back shelf.

CHAPTER FOURTEEN

Sound travels in this house. I can hear the clinking of silverware and muttered voices. Apparently, Domino and Alexi have carried on with their meal without me.

Somehow, I find that more unnerving than if he had hunted me down the hall and was banging on the door. It means that he's willing to make me wait, stewing in his anger and devising a crueler punishment.

The full extent of what I've done doesn't sink in until I parse over what I said to him—all within Alexi's earshot. If I truly wasn't supposed to know about his role in masterminding the twisted plot that got me here, well, then I'm about to find out.

Though, I can't feel too guilty for tarnishing his little ruse when I realize that Alexi let a secret of her own slip. Domino had her sleep with Tristan and was ready and waiting to take pictures.

Did he convince her during those sexy sessions between the

two of them that he also documented? All she had to do was "play her role."

It stings to think of him working with her—of the two of them plotting against my family and me. Even if I did cause a rift between him and Jaguar over his apparent deceit, I shouldn't care. Right?

I can't ignore the way he looked at me in the bathroom as blood dripped down my face. He seemed unguarded then, as though he had nothing to hide. Nothing left to lose.

What will he do if he thinks I've put a wrench in his carefully crafted plan?

I don't have to speculate for long.

I hear footsteps first, light initially, then firmer. Heavier. They advance slowly in this direction, as though the source of them has all the time in the world.

But the closer they come, the more anger becomes apparent in every steady, resonating footfall.

My heart starts to race as they grow nearer, eventually stopping where I assume the door to be. I hear a distinctive jangle as if they tested the doorknob, finding it locked.

I tense, expecting banging. A threat. Promises of violence.

Instead…

The steps retreat.

My confusion spurs me to creep from my hiding place, straining my ears for any other sound that might give me a clue of his next course of action. All I hear is silence, and the chirping of insects encroaching from outside. I must have left the window open.

But despite how hard I listen, I can't discern any noises that might be coming from inside the house. No footsteps. No voices, either Domino's or Alexi's.

No noise at all, except for my rapidly beating heart and the frantic sound of my own breathing.

Warily, I creep to the closet door and push it open—only to have it wrenched out of my grasp, flung from the outside.

Domino lurks behind it, though I don't believe my eyes at first. Behind him, the mattress and wardrobe are still positioned before the closed door. There's no way he could have gotten in.

Then I feel him—the heat of his breath against my temple as he exhales harshly. With one hand, he grips the doorway, blocking me in. His fingers shake, the knuckles stark white, his entire body resonating with tension.

"You have no fucking clue what you've done," he tells me, but his voice is worlds apart from the restrained growl he displayed in the dining room. It's nowhere close to his bellowed shouts or the angriest snarl I've heard him utilize. It's different. Colder. Softer. Like a whisper ripped from his chest, against his will. Something so hard for him to voice he can't believe he's actually doing so. "Do you?"

He releases the door and snags my chin, dragging me toward him. "You stupid, foolish…" He breaks off as if I'm not even worth the effort of insulting. "You've just fucked up everything I've spent five fucking years putting into motion. Again."

I flinch at that. It sounds like such an overreaction to one petty outburst. Alexi Rojas has the power to unravel the schemes of the great and powerful Domino Valenciaga? I wouldn't believe it if it weren't for his words that choose now to haunt me.

She works for him.

His eyes narrow, nostrils flaring. "Goddamn, I should just let him have you. You're not even worth the fucking effort of—"

"Maybe if you would stop lying to me," I croak, trying to wrench away. "I could actually *trust* you."

He tightens his grip, tugging me even closer. My breasts graze his chest, and through the heated skin, I swear I can feel his heart pounding. Pulsating. Raging.

He's so angry, and I can't resist this pathetic need to defend myself, even though I damn well shouldn't have to.

"You sent Alexi after Tristan."

He blinks, and I take advantage of the brief moment of distraction to pull away and stagger further into the closet, putting as much distance between us that I can.

"You told that whore to fuck my boyfriend, and then you took photo evidence as proof. For what? So you could get off on having both of us as your little pawns?"

"No." He shrugs the insinuation off, his expression cold. "I sent Alexi to Tristan to find out what he knew. Your father had been coy on his role in their little scheme. As it turns out, I had a damn good reason to be suspicious."

"My… My father?"

It doesn't make sense. There are too many strings composing this twisted web. I can't make heads or tails of it.

Domino advances a step, clenching his hands into fists at his sides. I can practically feel his restraint, causing a shift in the atmosphere like a building storm cloud just before the rain breaks loose.

"He was growing paranoid, Ada. Restless. A wild beast is always the most dangerous when it's cornered. When it feels its life is on the line. By that point, it will resort to any option it can to free itself. Like using its daughter as a pawn to throw off suspicion for its connection to a potential crime spree."

It's my turn to blink, caught off guard by the word choice.

"What are you even talking about?"

He scoffs. "Silly little Ada. Of course, you wouldn't take time from your shopping to educate yourself on something as trivial as your father being openly linked by the media to a sex trafficking ring."

I swallow hard, bristling at the disgust in his tone. "My father was about to be indicted for some silly hit and run," I say. "They didn't even have strong evidence against him. He was just being set up to take the fall so his enemies could run roughshod over his reputation."

I'm parroting exactly what my father told me—what he ranted and raved about for the last month before this mess even began. He needed me to use Tristan as a way into the prosecutor's case, though he wasn't assigned to it. Somehow, he still knew enough information to make those shitty, unmemorable nights with him worth it to my father. Enough that he kept pushing me to meet with him.

And maybe, I liked the attention. I liked knowing that, despite having someone as beautiful as Alexi to screw around with, he still desired me—even if it was because of my proximity to my father. I still won.

It's so silly now to think about that. I feel my cheeks flame, and I almost miss Domino's reaction to that statement. Rather than look shocked or satisfied that I at least knew something about the case, he frowns.

"What was the man's name?"

"What?"

"The man who died, what was his name?" He makes his tone flat, speaking deliberately slow.

"I don't know. Some jogger, I think—"

"Some jogger." He laughs, raking a hand through his dark hair. "Try some businessman that authorities had been trailing for six months as part of a sting operation to catch the ringleader of a sex trafficking ring that stretches from

Terra Rodea to halfway across the country. That man dies and so does the investigation and the only link they had to finding a mastermind. Unless they could put pressure on the suspect who might have wanted that man dead, even if they had flimsy fucking evidence."

"My father?"

"*Bingo*, as they say, Ada-Maria. I know you rarely left that mansion of yours, but I would think you'd have access to the internet, at least."

"What does that have to do with me?"

"Think." He takes another step, and I hit my shoulder on a shelf in my haste to retreat. As the wall meets my back, I realize that I'm trapped. There's nowhere left to go. "Who stands to benefit if you happened to be kidnapped —let alone murdered—in a violent raid on some fancy restaurant? Maybe the man desperate to prove to the police and the world that he isn't connected to the same ring that might have stolen his only daughter? It's a sloppy plan, but desperate times call for desperate measures, Ada. Tell me that I don't have to spell it out for you."

"You're lying," I snap. And I have plenty of reason to doubt him, stemming from his own cruel attempts at manipulating me. Besides, I remember something else from the night I was taken. "The indictment was being called off. Tristan told me. They weren't going to make an arrest."

Domino's brows knit together with a swiftness that makes me suspect he didn't know that tidbit of information. Just when I start to believe that might be true, he shrugs.

"I wonder what else did Tristan tell you? That he was fucking multiple other women? That he was working with your father behind your back? That you were just a steppingstone on his own ambitious career path?"

"And maybe I should have appreciated him more," I croak. "Because he at least pretended to give a damn about me. Which is more than I can say for you. You want me to be worried that I ruined your little plan, Domino? Well, I'm not. You've yet to prove that you're any better than the hell you claim awaits me. A hell you sold me to—"

"Sir?" The quiet voice, paired with a delicate series of knocks on the door, seems so out of place amid this tension that I lose my train of thought.

Raising his voice, Domino heads into the bedroom. "Yes, Ines?"

"Mr. Jaguar will arrive tomorrow afternoon," she says. "I will make the necessary arrangements."

"Thank you." Domino waits until her soft steps retreat down the hall before he turns to me, snatching my wrist.

"You doubt me? Well, now you'll get to see firsthand if you've made the right choice or not. Don't you realize?" He yanks me to him, staring me down with eyes like fire. "I can't protect you this time, Ada-Maria."

"This time?" I echo hoarsely. "When have you ever protected me? Even once?"

He slams his free hand against my jaw with barely enough restraint to keep from hurting me. He merely forces my head to the side, inspecting me from this newer angle. It provides him the chance to lower his mouth to my ear without breaking eye contact.

"When have I protected you? From the second I set foot in that fucking house, my only focus *was* you."

He shoves me aside, and I trip, landing on my knee. As I scramble to regain my balance, I realize exactly how he got in.

One of the large, French-style windows is open, letting in the warm night air. He must have come through it. But why?

The easiest explanation is that he wanted to catch me off guard, but I think it's more than that, lurking in the reality that a man like him would have no problem breaking through my barriers. Easily.

The only reason he'd circumvent the more violent action is if he wanted to avoid making a scene—and exposing Alexi to his more ferocious nature.

God, I don't know why the thought stings. It's so stupid to take offense to his apparent awareness of her. She's his accomplice, after all.

"You never cared about me," I say, eyeing one of the many scrapes on my legs that prove that point. "I was an idiot to believe you'd ever keep your word."

"No," he growls, advancing toward me. "It's your turn to keep your word."

A rustling sound catches the air, and I brace for a blow. Instead, something lands against the floor within my reach. I have to blink just to make sure it's really here.

He must have had it on him all this time, at least during dinner. Pia's diary.

If Jaguar's impending visit has him on edge, then why choose now to bring up the past again?

Because he believes this will be his only chance, a concern that should definitely add strength to the "jaguar is no better than he is," column.

"You think Pia's at the house. Her house. Why?"

"It was a guess—"

"You're not that naïve, Ada," he snarls. "Neither am I."

He appears before me, crouched on one knee, his expression like ice, each rugged feature etched in stone. "Give me a reason to believe there might be something in that empty skull of yours worth salvaging."

I can't escape the feeling that he's proposing the dare like a test. Make him value me. Give him something worth saving. Cower and beg.

"You never knew her very well," I say, matching his soft tone. "Your sister. Because if you did, you wouldn't seem so puzzled by the breadcrumb trail she left behind. That's what she did, Domino. She kept secrets. She fed on lies."

"And you seemed to have learned plenty from her." He stands, crossing his arms, staring down at me with a glare so piercing I go numb in the face of it. "You're more selfish than I gave you credit for. Too fucking spoiled to even consider what might be for your own fucking good."

"So tell me, then," I counter, jutting my chin. "Stop dancing around in circles and just tell me what kind of danger I'm in. Tell me the truth about everything—"

"The truth?" He inclines his head sharply, his eyes narrowing to slits. "The truth, Ada-Maria, is that Jaguar doesn't see you as some worthless pawn through which he can control your father. That's just a bonus. He sees you as…"

"What?" I demand, unnerved by how his voice deepens and his eyes take on a faraway gleam. It's as if he's staring a million years into the past, rooted here by sheer force of will.

"Jaguar sees you as a way to get to me," he says. "And he'll do that however he can. He'll hurt you. Violate you. Anything he can think of to keep me in line."

He doesn't sound like he's lying, but I can't square that description of me with a man who's done all those things to me himself. Hurt. Violate. Anything he can think of. A part of me questions if it's just jealousy that has him so on edge. Even so, I'm not sure if I'm brave enough to be at the mercy of someone else.

"Who is he to you?"

He stiffens, his teeth gritted. Again, he tears his hand through his hair, turning his back to me as he starts to pace. "He is… No one," he declares, looking down on me from over his shoulder. "No one that will interest you, anyway. But congratulations, Ada-Maria, you've gotten your wish— someone seeks to use you beyond just getting to your father. Congratulations. I can't save you this time."

CHAPTER FIFTEEN

"You have a funny definition of that word. Saving," I point out, too exhausted to take offense. In so many ways, this man is a stranger in comparison to the steady, comforting presence I've known him as for the past five years—at the same time, he's terrifyingly familiar. His secretive, manipulative ways and penchant for brutality remind me of someone I knew better than anyone else on the planet.

My father. Domino picked up way more from his time with "Don Roy" than he seems to realize. They're utterly the same.

"It seems like *you've* gotten your wish," I counter, bracing my hand against the floor in an attempt to rise to my feet. "Jaguar gets to hurt me, torture me. Whether with you or with him, it looks like I only have agony to look forward to—"

"I am nothing like him," he growls, his voice rippling like thunder, and yet still low enough that I doubt he penetrates the walls of this room, even with the window open. He turns on his heel and yanks me to my feet, capturing my chin with one hand. "I'll give you something he never would, Ada. Mercy—" Roughly, he scrapes the hair back from my face, leaving nothing in the way of his gaze meeting mine. "You want my protection now? Then beg me for it."

I'd laugh if he didn't sound and look so damn serious. There's no hint of amusement glinting in those disarming eyes, no mocking in his tone.

"I'd rather die."

"That can be arranged," he says without an ounce of hesitation. His fingers twitch as if to reinforce the dark intent glinting in his eyes. He'd have no problem at all "arranging" that ending for me—but only on his terms. "Fortunately for you, I still need you before then, and Jaguar won't be so accommodating. Beg me to help you like a good girl," he coaxes in a gritty baritone. Using his grip on my chin, he manipulates my head so that his mouth is near my ear again. "Use those sweet words and that sexy little pout. Tell me that I'm all you ever wanted. Spin those little lies about how I earned your gratitude forever just by dragging you off a fucking highway. Make me believe it, little Ada. Lie sweetly about how much you need me, and maybe I'll be convinced."

I can't even put into words how much it hurts to have him mock me like this. It's comparable to having a rusty, filthy nail puncture wound that never fully healed over and over again.

I could deny I ever gave a damn about him. Spit in his face. Lie.

Instead, I strain his grasp until I'm staring directly into his eyes. "I wanted the person I thought you were; I have no shame in admitting that," I confess, feeling my upper lip pull back from my teeth. I'll get nothing out of sinking down to his level, but I don't care. It feels strangely good to speak this openly to him. Damn mind games and verbal tricks. "I wanted the Domino I considered brave and honorable. I would have given that man anything. My body. My heart. My soul. You can laugh at me for that if you want. Joke and make taunts. That doesn't matter. The truth is still this—you never had to brutalize me, Domino. You could have told me anything, and I would have believed you. You didn't need Alexi to get to Tristan. I would have told you whatever you wanted to know. I could have been yours with so much less effort, and if you played your cards right, you would have never needed to spin a lie for Jaguar or anyone else. Wholeheartedly, I would have trusted you. That makes *you* the fool, not me."

His eyes darken as he processes that speech, and I expect him to scoff in disbelief. Deny it. Make another low dig at my expense.

Instead, he tilts his head thoughtfully as if giving serious consideration to every alleged claim. It's so surreal being on the receiving end of one of these appraising glances. Usually, he'd look at my father this way while trying to figure out how to best implement one of his many orders.

"Maybe you think you're telling the truth," he deduces finally, in a voice like sin. Hell itself. "Maybe… But it's my turn to let you know something, Ada-Maria." He strokes down to my throat and toys with my windpipe, applying varying amounts of pressure. Soft at first. Then harder. Harder… "Maybe I didn't want to be put on a pedestal based on your childish, unrealistic expectations. What if I wanted more than that? What if I needed to shatter your fantasy of me and make you squirm, see how you react under pressure, get to run that smart fucking mouth with no regard for the paparazzi or your daddy's wishes. What if I wanted to see you despair at your rock bottom to know if you were even wort—" He bites off the rest, and I can sense the tension in what he doesn't want to say.

"Worthy of what?" I demand.

He shoves me back so hard I go flying. Only the wall can break the momentum, and breathless, I brace my hands against it, struggling to get my bearings.

He advances on me slowly, sizing me up with a ruthless, raking glance. He comes toe to toe with me, palming the wall on either side of my body, using his weight as effectively as prison bars to keep me boxed in.

When his mouth finds my ear again, he bites down on the lobe. Hard.

"That you were worthy of being the only woman on my fucking mind for the past five years."

My throat goes dry, thoughts utterly blank. This man doesn't sound like Domino, or even the monster I've been faced with since coming here. No, he is a new creature entirely, one who radiates possession in every single word ripped from his throat.

"That you were worthy of having me wonder what you taste like. What you fucking smell like. I've obsessed over this body, Ada-Maria. What I would have you wear when you were mine. How I would bathe you. Fuck you. Command you. I've imagined a million goddamn times how that ass would feel in the palms of my hands. The look on your face when you finally realized you were mine. Always mine, meant to be claimed since the moment I first saw you in Don Roy's office. Or maybe I just like toying with you," he adds in a guttural rasp, bringing one of his hands to my throat. Cold, his eyes spear through me, as violently as that blade he carries. "Maybe I like seeing that fragile, pathetic hope bubble in your eyes that you might be something more than the warm, wet hole Roy Pavalos could pimp out to further his own aims. You make it so fucking easy."

I gasp. Or maybe it's a sob? By now, I should be so accustomed to his mind games that nothing he said could ever hurt me. But it does.

He does. And his nostrils flare as if savoring the scent of that pain.

"In fact, I could just tell you everything," he adds. "You wouldn't even know what to believe or not. Like maybe I do remember that night on the road, Ada-Maria. I remember how fucking angry I was to see you there. I could have wrapped my hands around your throat then and there, and your papa would be none the wiser. What if I always sensed you beyond the trees at night? I could smell you on the wind even if I never saw you… Or hell, maybe I was the one watching *you*, following Don Roy's orders to an extent, but everything beyond that was of my own volition. I'd see you with those men, hunt you down while you were alone with them. Sneak a glimpse of you in any way that I could and memorize every inch of that body. You'd never know the fucking difference."

He's right, and my head is spinning, trying to keep up with his many twisted narratives. The only way to salvage what little sanity I have left is to close my eyes, blocking him out.

The second I do, he applies more pressure to the hand he has around my neck. Enough to make my eyes bulge, my lids springing open again.

"You were always mine, Ada-Maria. You just never realized it. You still don't—not the lengths I will go through to keep you mine. The harm I will do to any man who dares to defile you. Take you. Harm you. You looked at your fantasy Domino with childish love once, but frankly, Ada, you have no idea what that concept means. None. Love is agony, you see. It is cruel obsession. It leaves no choice in whether you want it or not. It is all-consuming. So when I tell you to beg me to keep you, I want you to realize that you already have. Just by listening to me now with that hungry look on your face. Just by humoring the feel of my body next to yours and letting me shove my tongue inside of that greedy pussy. From day one, you've been begging."

He strokes my cheek in a motion that feels cruelly gentle. Then he tilts my head and lowers his mouth to mine.

The kiss catches me off guard, firm and possessive.

My thoughts scatter, common sense far beyond my reach— so it's entirely out of reflex that I sink my teeth into his tongue. Rather than recoil, he grunts, leaning into the motion, making it a part of the kiss itself. I taste blood as he sucks at me. Devours me.

Somehow, I release him, knowing I need to break away. Push him off. Run.

His hands are already gliding down my hips, drawing me into him. I'm breathless when our lips finally pull apart, but he's the one in control of the action, blood smeared across his lower lip.

"I don't need to hear it," he reiterates gruffly, in between heavy pants. "But I want to—beg me to protect you."

I use both hands to push against his chest, but he doesn't budge. "Go to hell."

"Gladly." He pushes back, forcing my hands aside as he brings his mouth within inches of my own. "I'll meet you there. Because what we are, Ada? It sure ain't heavenly." He runs his thumb across my mouth, thrusting it between my lips without warning. "It's sinful."

I spit him out and contemplate slapping him again. Instead, I say, "We aren't anything, and I'll never beg you for a damn thing. Except to let me go."

"And you might get your wish." His expression shifts, becoming even more indecipherable than I'm used to. He is all shadow and gold. "You are an expensive woman to keep, far more than you know."

He lets that cryptic phrase hang in the air as he turns away, his shoulders rigid. "It would be easier to let him have you. Far better in the long run. And you…" He looks back at me, his eyes dark and shadowed. "You're so good at fucking pretending, you wouldn't even notice, would you? If he were touching you instead of me—" He's back, dragging me against him no matter how violently I resist. My nails dig into his forearms, and I kick, wincing as the sores on my feet throb at full force. He's unmovable, easily able to maneuver me away from the wall, across the room. "You wouldn't care if he were fucking you. You'd make those little noises, and bite your lip and ride him as though he were a fucking king—" He shoves me back, and I land on the box spring, gaping up at him as he looms above. "Can you even tell the difference, Ada-Maria? Between the cock of a bastard you despise, and the one of the man who worships this little body from the inside out?"

His hands land on my thighs, applying enough force to flatten them against the box spring. My heart starts to race, my throat suddenly dry. His shift in tone is giving me whiplash. Emotionless one minute, dark and gritted the next…

"Can you even tell the difference between pleasure and pain?" He crouches, running one of his hands along my thigh.

I kick at him, attempting to clamp my knees together. He drags them apart, pulling me to the edge of the bed so that my legs are on either side of him, perched against his hips.

"Can you tell the difference between fucking a man who doesn't give a damn about you and one who craves every fucking inch of your body?"

Yes, a part of me whispers, pairing the way Tristan would touch me to…

"I used to imagine it," he tells me, holding my legs captive. "Having you at my mercy like this. Mine alone."

My only mode to attack him is to rear up and lash at his chest, nails drawn. Every blow, he withstands without flinching. When I aim for his face next, he hooks his fingers around the back of my skull, wrenching me toward him. As a result, I'm forced almost onto my knees, chest pressed against him as he claims my mouth again.

This time, I don't go down without a fight. I bite, scratching at any inch of exposed skin. He groans, swallowing each attempt at aggression. Like he's getting off on it all. My fight. My hate. The fact that there's nowhere I can go.

He has me, body and soul. Not by choice.

He's too strong, his lips like fire, lashing me open and igniting any flesh he comes in contact with. Against my will, I groan for him, letting him eagerly drink down the sound.

Then I remember my senses and bite him again, so hard he pulls back.

"I will never be yours," I hiss, startled by the intensity in my own voice. "So sell me if you want to. You can't hurt me."

No more than he already has, at least.

He makes a low sound in the back of his throat as he shoves me down. This time, he mounts me after, pinning my limbs to the bed, all while distributing his weight so as to not hurt me. A part of me marvels at that, though I can't tell if it's actual concern on his part.

Or merely so he has easy access to snatch a fistful of my skirt and drag it up over my waist.

"I *can* hurt you," he clarifies, and the look in his eye bolsters that warning. "But I can also give you more pleasure than any other man. You know that. Just in case, I should refresh your memory..."

He lunges, using one hand to pry my legs apart for his mouth to assault me again. Somehow, I'm still sensitive from the first time, and the shock of his warm lips nudging me apart renders me senseless. For one pathetic, brutal, beautiful second, I forget how much I should hate him, and I merely relent to the overwhelming wave of sensation he arouses with just one brush of his tongue.

And a thrust.

And another.

Another…

My back arches as my nails scrape at the unyielding material beneath me. Even it isn't a sturdy enough anchor. Desperate, I reach for something stronger and find it in the form of silk attached to a firm surface.

A "surface" that growls when I flex my nails against it. Hurting him is my only form of retaliation as he torments me with every stroke of his tongue.

The orgasm I can feel building coils in my stomach, growing stronger and stronger until I'm swallowed by it.

"Jesus Christ," he hisses as I writhe, my body convulsing.

I think the whiplash is too much, even for him. He rises onto his knees, his lips glistening, gaze seeking out mine.

I'm still gasping for air when I realize what he's doing—not retreating, just wrenching his pants down his legs, freeing a cock that stabs proudly at the air, already fully erect.

I think I try to say something. Refuse. Mock him. Deny him.

Any sound dies in my throat as he guides my legs apart, entering me with one swift thrust.

I take him deeper than I can stand. So deep my head rears back, and I swear I can feel him forcing his way up my throat. There's nothing gentle about the way he takes me.

He grinds with his hips, forcing his cock into my furthest depths with a boldness no one has ever dared utilize before. Like he truly believes what he said—he owns me. He's studied me. He knows me.

And all I can do is take every inch he has to give.

CHAPTER SIXTEEN

I hate the feeling of his breath on my breasts. Even if I don't move to escape the punishing bursts of heat, I hate it. I hate how he holds me after, like he didn't just insult me moments ago. Like the feel of my body in his arms is enough to please a man like him.

Someone so violent, so vicious.

I despise the way he can lull me into a false sense of security before I even realize it. Only when his nostrils flare, and his brows furrow do I remember where we are. Who I am.

And what he's done.

"What are you doing?" I ask him in a whisper.

That simple question flips a switch in him. "My Ada," he growls, shoving me from his chest as he rolls onto his side, putting his back to me. "Still begging."

I don't bother to deny him. I'm too tired. I merely lie back, looking up at the ceiling and count the many ways I've let him regain the upper hand again.

On second thought, denying him is the only modicum of power I have left. Still, not in the outright sense of the word. It's more subtle than that, lurking in all the things he hasn't said just yet.

"Why *Domino?*" I ask of the darkness surrounding us, so thick I can only see the outline of his muscular back, ghosted by a hint of pale light coming in through the windows. "Why that name?"

It's so long before he so much as sighs in response. I think he won't reply at all.

"Because Navid Inglecias is dead," he says, startling me.

At first, I think literally—that he's revealing yet another twist to this wicked plot he's set into motion. Then I realize that he would sound far smugger if that were the case.

Not…exhausted.

"He died of a congenital heart condition," he adds. "The poor bastard."

"Why pick Domino?" I ask, though I'm not sure why I'm even curious. His origin means nothing as it relates to my ultimate fate. One he seems resigned to.

"If you were listening closely, Ada, I think you might be able to put the pieces together all by yourself."

I bristle at the brush-off. Then I remember a name he mentioned once. *Domin… Domingas.*

"Carlos Domingas," I say. "Did you pick the name as an homage to him?"

"Again, you prove that you are nowhere near as dumb as you pretend to be," he says.

A compliment? "I don't think even Don Roy made that connection."

I can see how the name would appeal to someone like him. He could rub his true allegiance in the face of his enemy from the start. Considering how long my father kept him around, maybe he never made the connection at all.

"What about Valenciaga?"

I expect that he won't answer directly or spin another riddle at my expense.

"My mother…"

Something in my chest gives way, startling me at the intensity of the emotion. Is this sympathy? When applied to him, I can't tell.

I don't remember Mrs. Inglecias much. Just that she was a kind, beautiful woman with dark hair and warm brown eyes. Pia spoke of her rarely, but I got the sense she respected her in a way I never would my own mother.

"Her mother's maiden name," he adds, his voice gruff. "An obscure enough distinction to hopefully go unnoticed by Roy Pavalos."

He put a lot of thought into this, I realize. He had to in order to go five years undetected. The level of depth is mind-blowing, especially when I consider the trajectory of my life during the same amount of time. I lived in my parents' home, on my father's dime, and I implicitly trusted any man he brought into our orbit. Before now, if I had been forced to guess which of my father's associates would have betrayed him, Domino would have been at the very bottom of the list. I would have never imagined he could be Navid, either. Namely for one reason.

"Your heart? How did you afford it?" I ask, rolling on my side. The box spring isn't as forgiving as the mattress would be, and the material protests in grating creaks with every movement.

He sighs. "I'll humor you, Ada-Maria. Would you like the long version or the short?"

I'm surprisingly curious to hear any ounce of information he'll give, but I'm not foolish enough to waste his amicable mood on one story.

"Short," I say, to play it safe and hope he hasn't grown bored of me yet.

"As a favor to my mother, a kind, mysterious benefactor gave it to me out of the goodness of his heart. How is that explanation?"

"A lie," I suspect. "No one does anything out of the goodness of their heart."

Not even him, apparently.

"I'll let you put the pieces together," he says, cryptic once again. "In the meantime, I suggest you shut that pretty mouth of yours, unless it's to beg."

Because Jaguar is coming tomorrow.

And I have no idea what that heralds for me.

CHAPTER SEVENTEEN

I wake up to the sensation of warm sun on my back and the feeling of an empty bed, over which I'm lying lengthwise, my feet dangling off the edge. I know without having to open my eyes that Domino is gone.

Maybe I'm too fucking pathetic to check for myself. I don't need any confirmation to reinforce the coolness of the box spring beneath me or the lack of thick, brutal fingers raking through my hair.

And I can hear his voice…

Faint, it sounds like it's coming from beyond the room, but not in the direction of the hall. The closet?

"…be ready for me. I know it's earlier than we planned. Just be fucking ready. I have no idea what he'll do; just wait for my signal. *Gracias.*"

Curiosity alone spurs me to open my eyes, just in time to catch him storming from the closet, a cell phone in hand.

My gaze latches onto it for a second before my brain sleepily catches up, and I realize why the sight strikes me as so odd.

I've heard him on the phone, but I rarely see him with it. In fact, the last time Jaguar called, Ines brought the phone to *him*. He must be keeping it hidden somewhere beyond my reach.

Just in case, I decided to do the smart thing, like call for help or try to figure out where in the hell we actually are.

"Get up." He meets my gaze while stowing the phone in his pocket—a spot where I know for a fact that he doesn't keep the device regularly.

As if aware of me watching, he gathers the clothing scattered across the floor one item at a time.

"Go wash yourself and get dressed," he tells me, tugging at his collar. Today, it's buttoned all the way, the closest he's come to embodying the dress style he utilized while working for my family.

Is it merely coincidence that today happens to be the day Jaguar has made it known that he'll arrive? I'm not bold enough to jump to that conclusion. Yet.

Instead, I scramble to my feet, still naked. I catch his eyes raking over me, and I note that they gleam as coldly as his tone. It's a subtle, but disarming change from his relaxed mood last night. Once again, I have whiplash at how volatile he can be. Calm, like a sheet of ice one minute, and blazing the next to rival the most intense inferno.

Staggering to my feet, I slip past him, eagerly darting into the closet. I can't escape the tension weighing down the atmosphere. I can taste the unease. The dread.

In so many ways, it reminds me of those brief moments when my father would be away on business, right before his return. The faint smile my mother would sport in his absence would fade, and the servants would become frantic, ensuring every little detail was in place.

On second thought, it's not exactly the same. Jaguar inspires something in Domino that not even my father seemed to. In the presence of Roy, he was always the stoic bodyguard, despite his supposed hatred of us from the very beginning.

But when it comes to Jaguar, or Julian, there is no ounce of restraint that I can sense. He's shamelessly angry, uncaring of who sees it.

As hilarious as a comparison it might be, in my head, I'm bold enough to make it. When it comes to Jaguar, Domino reminds me of…

Well, me. Trapped in a world, he has no clue of how to escape. All he can do is go through the motions and loathe every minute of it.

But therein lies a murkier set of questions that I'm not even sure I want to toy with speculating on. My father had twenty-five years to break me down and mold me into the creature I've become. In essence, that time has numbed me to all of the vile things he's made me do. Some of them, anyway.

But what has Jaguar made Domino do to garner such hatred? For the past five years, he's spent nearly every waking moment in Terra Rodea? Does their feud stem from before that, maybe around the time he received his mysterious transplant?

I'll let you put the pieces together, he said last night. I thought it was a cruel jab at first, but now I can parse over all of the other little breadcrumbs he's let slip. Once, he told me that he owes a debt that can't be paid with paper money—only blood.

How did he put it? *An eye for an eye. A tooth for a tooth.*

A heart for a heart.

I brush my fingers along my chest and realize I'm shaking, even before my newest suspicion has fully taken hold. Could Jaguar's interest in me go beyond sex? He bought my "body," but in the literal sense…

"I told you to get dressed."

I turn, startled by the sight of him still here. His gaze flits over me, dark and unreadable. Any other moment, I don't think I'd be brave enough to provoke him so early.

But, as it turns out, I might not have much time left to find answers of my own.

"You sold me," I croak, hating the raw pain in my voice—and the fear. "Be honest. You didn't sell me to some sex dungeon, did you?"

"I don't follow," he replies.

"Did you sell my…b-body. You said you owed Jaguar more than money. Did he find your heart? And now you've promised him a new one."

He laughs, and I blink at the sound; it's rich. Almost as real as the one he displayed with Alexi. As he chuckles, he enters the closet again, and my own heart stutters.

"You think I've sold your body parts on some transplant black market? That's too creative, Ada-Maria, even for me."

"So then clarify it and stop dancing around the truth."

His eyes cut to slits. "I sold you to be fucked and tossed from buyer to buyer. Use your imagination to fill in the gaps." He might as well be referring to an animal. Or a bug. Something he deems beneath the need for empathy.

An object.

I don't know which ultimate ending would be worse, to be honest. To be used for sex or sliced to pieces. Either way, it's obvious that he doesn't give a damn.

"Maybe you should wrap me with a bow," I whisper, feeling so helpless… I could scream. "Then I'll be ready either way."

"I'd tie the bow around your neck," he suggests. "*Then* you would be ready either way. Now get dressed."

He stalks past me and snatches a dress from a hanger. Then he reenters the main room and approaches the makeshift barricade still blocking the door. With graceful ease, he shoves the mattress aside and pushes the wardrobe back to its usual spot.

Opening the door, he leads the way into the hall and into the bathroom. Then he runs the water in the tub, and when he reaches for me, I can tell from the set of his shoulders that he expects me to run or put up a fight.

I don't do either, letting him drag me into the water with no resistance.

I submit to the surprisingly warm—not scalding—bath and barely pay him any attention as he retreats to the other end of the room.

I'm too busy dwelling on the current state of my life. In retrospect, could I have ever expected to end up any differently? Still a pawn of my father's, despite what Domino claims. It's hate for Roy Pavalos that darkens his gaze every time he looks at me.

"You have that look," Domino scolds, reappearing with a towel that he places on the floor, a rag, and a bar of soap. Sinking into a crouch, he dips the rag into the water and works it into a lather. "That pining, kicked-puppy look that warns Ada-Maria hasn't gotten her way."

"I'm not in the mood for jokes," I say absently, staring straight ahead even as I feel the water swish as a result of his ministrations. "I'm thinking of how sad your life must be. Five years. All this effort, and my father is hooked up to a machine keeping him alive, and I'm 'at your mercy.' And yet, you don't seem very happy, Domino. You could have done so much more rather than gain so little. All in the name of revenge."

"How many times do I have to say it?"

A gasp catches in my throat as the warmth of the rag strokes over my chest, guided by his hand. He makes the motion brusque on purpose, I suspect. I've seen men wash a car with more care.

"This was always about more than just you or your father."

I finally look at him. He's hunched over the tub, seemingly intent on dragging the cloth down over my belly before moving to the part of my thigh exposed above the water's surface.

"Then why work so hard to infiltrate us?" I demand. I sound angrier than I have the energy to feel. If he did it all for no reason, then that makes him less dangerous mastermind and more… Callous, sloppily cruel for no reason. "Why arrange for my mother to be killed. Why—"

"I'll tell you a story, Ada-Maria." He tosses the rag aside and braces his hands against the rim of the tub. "A story about a stupid, poor boy with a broken heart who made a deal with the devil because he believed life was worth living, enough to fight for it, no matter the cost. Then he quickly realized what men like Roy Pavalos take for granted. Some bargains aren't worth the price you wind up paying. Life, as wonderful as it may be, isn't worth selling your soul to maintain, and sometimes the consequences for hunting down wealth and power, no matter the cost, can be heftier than anyone is willing to pay. You may sob for your father, all while forgetting the hell he put countless other people through. The dozens of papas and mamas he stole, the families and lives he ruined. And yet, as twisted as he may be, Ada-Maria, he is but a tiny cog in the wheel of evil men who keep this cruel world turning. I suggest you dry your tears, because this is only the beginning."

I am crying, though I didn't even realize. It's like my eyes have been so overworked these past few days; they drip without any warning or input from my brain, painting warm trails down my cheeks.

I try to garner any meaning that I can from his little story—that my father is just one in a long line of men he plans to ruin? A part of me doesn't care, and doesn't want to waste any more time trying to understand the complexities of Domino Valenciaga. It's the same impulse that used to drive me to drugs—a vicious need to ignore my life and current surroundings no matter the cost.

I embrace it now, putting everything else out of my mind but a desire for quiet. I ignore him, leaning back to wet my hair beneath the water. Then I submerge myself fully beneath the surface, drowning out the world. And him.

He's still speaking, I realize, as a rumble of syllables reaches me, distorted by the water. I contemplate ignoring him, using that as an excuse to stay under, long past the moment my lungs start screaming for air, and the blood rushes through my skull…

Finally, I sit up again, gulping for breath.

But he's still speaking, unperturbed by my interruption. "…and what if this boy made a bargain without knowing there was a price to pay at first," he says softly. "He merely wanted to live and cease being a burden to those who loved him. He lived his borrowed life like a good soldier, staying within the confines of his new identity. But then he realized that it's suffocating as hell being forced to live a life you never asked for. You start to believe that you'll do anything to escape it. Kill anyone. But everything in life comes with a price, one that must be paid."

I'm holding my breath again. He sounds different than before. I suspect this story is less hypothetical than he led me to believe, and I scramble to listen, inspecting every word and the picture they paint. Domino believes himself to be that boy, I think. He made a deal with the devil —Jaguar?

And now he's paying the price.

"So to cancel your debt, you sacrifice me?" I ask him, gathering the nerve to meet his gaze. I expect to find the same bold, mocking man I've been battling with all morning, poised to deliver an insult at my expense.

"No."

The figure I'm faced with now is a man I've almost forgotten he used to be these past few days. The stoic, cold Domino Valenciaga with a wealth of secrets hidden behind that searching stare. Even without the aid of his cowboy hat, his mystery returns in full force—and I can't escape the feeling that I'm only seeing a fraction of the real danger he's thrust me into. Only what he wants me to see.

"No, Ada-Maria." He plunges his hand beneath the water's surface, skirting my parted legs, to withdraw the rag. Deliberately, he takes time wringing out every drop of moisture from it. "You haven't been paying attention. If selling your cunt could save the world, Tristan Lucas would be a very happy, very alive, and very wealthy man. You have value only to the right people. The right kind of men."

I'm more frustrated than ever. It feels like he's spinning me around and around, taking immense satisfaction in watching me squirm and question. He loves keeping me blind and off-balance.

What's the point of even attempting to resist him? Why not give him exactly what he wants?

"I want you to protect me," I ask him directly. "I'm asking you to."

I expect him to grin evilly over the prospect of me pleading for help. Instead, he frowns, his eyes narrowing.

"I was wrong," he says, rising to his feet. "Begging doesn't look good on you. Get up."

I obey, letting him dry me off and dress me in the outfit he procured from the closet—a black dress with spaghetti straps and a neckline low enough to rival Alexi's.

I wonder where she is. Has she left now that Jaguar is arriving? Was she the one who called him in the first place?

"I'm sorry if I caused a rift between you and your little friend," I say, as he withdraws from me and heads for the hall.

"Don't be." The look he shoots over his shoulder is eerily calm. Composed. Too composed when paired with his rage from last night. "You did exactly what was expected of you."

He leaves without grunting out a command, and I don't race to follow him. Damn the smug bastard. He has my head spinning again. Just what was he hinting at? That he knew I would lose my cool around Alexi and blow up his little plan? Then why tell me to keep quiet in the first place?

Because he's lying, obviously. He didn't plan this, or he wouldn't have been on the phone earlier, confessing to a change in timeline. But that just brings up the bigger question of what exactly he is planning.

And why.

I must lose track of time, because the next time I startle to awareness, my hair is nearly dry, and Ines is standing in the doorway to the bathroom.

"Mr. Domino requests you join him for lunch," she says with a respectful nod. "He is on the terrace."

My heart pulses as I move to obey, entering the circular foyer to find that it's mid-morning already, if not the early afternoon. Domino is lounging alone this time, a platter of food on the table nearby.

I square my shoulders before stepping out from the archway, prepared to do battle yet again.

Instead, he gestures to the seat across from him. "Eat."

It's strange how he's broken down the one bastion of control I've ever maintained in my life. Hunger has always been a beast of my own making, always at my discretion for how gnawing it could become before I'd finally give into it.

Around him, hunger means nothing but a tool with which he can use to escalate any standoff to his advantage.

So I sit and snatch something from the tray at random, bringing it to my lips. I chew woodenly, holding his gaze for as long as I dare. When I finally look away, I hear the cushions of his lounger creak beneath his weight as if he shifted his position.

"Alexi was a pawn brought in by Jaguar to help me navigate the more delicate intricacies of the Terra Rodea social scene."

In other words, to fuck the men in my orbit.

"Why are you telling me this now?" I ask, glancing at him again.

He leans forward, staring past me, his expression harder than ever. "She fed me intel and kept me updated on the whereabouts of Tristan Lucas, but that was as far as our relationship extended. I never fucked her."

There's no inflection in his voice, and I can't tell if he's lying or telling the truth. All I can do is reiterate, "Why tell me this now?"

"Because Alexi belongs to Jaguar," he says coldly. "She always has. Everything she does, she reports back to him. I don't know what he has over her, so in some ways, I can't blame her. But you need to keep that in mind the next time you get the urge to run your mouth because I've pissed you off. Beyond your father's fancy mansion, everyone belongs to someone, Ada. The world is a patchwork of alliances and rivalries, and I suggest you think long and hard about who you align yourself with."

"How would someone like Alexi wind up with someone like Jaguar?" I ask.

He raises an eyebrow. I've surprised him, I think, but only because he seems to believe the question is too obvious to humor. "Why else?" He snatches a piece of fruit from the platter and takes a bite. Its juices paint his lips red as he declares, "People will do anything for love, or for revenge."

Is that his way of telling me that Alexi's motives stem back to what happened ten years ago? On the one hand, it sounds ridiculous. On the other…

After seeing the lengths Domino himself has gone through in the name of vengeance, I can't count out anything anymore.

"What does that mean? You alone can help me? Pardon me if I'm skeptical of that."

"You can be skeptical," he warns, taking another bite of fruit. "And still be smart. Tonight, you'll need to make a choice."

"You? So you can spin more riddles and torment me with even more mind games?"

"So I can find my sister's body," he counters in a tone so serious it catches me off guard. "And so you can tell me what really happened to her and stop using the missing pages of a diary as an excuse to feign ignorance. I want the truth from you. I'd prefer if you cooperate, but even if you decide to jump on Jaguar's cock tonight, know that I will still have you."

"Because you own me?" I ask softly, rephrasing the same claim he made against Alexi when it comes to Jaguar.

"No." Finished with his meal, he licks his fingertips clean. "Because you are not as stupid as you look. Sooner or later, you'll come crawling to me, and this time your begging won't be for show."

He thumbs my cheek and stands, wiping his hands on his pants.

"I'll be gone until tonight. Play nice, and I suggest you don't get tempted to go running into the desert again, either."

"Where are you going?" It's a bold question, one he humors with merely a raised eyebrow instead of an outburst of rage.

"A place where naughty girls, daughters of a monster like Roy Pavalos, can't follow. Ines will keep an eye on you, so don't get any ideas."

He strolls past me, entering the house, and I somehow can sense the exact moment he leaves. The tension in the air lessens, and I can breathe easier.

But in his absence, that ominous feeling from before only grows.

Jaguar is coming, and despite Domino's word games, I'm not sure what it means. Something bad, my intuition warns. I would be a fool to sit around and wait patiently for my impending doom to be handed to me on a silver platter.

I rise and enter the house, surprised to find no one wandering the spacious halls. Not Ines, or even Alexi. Is the blond still here? I can't sense her presence the way I can Domino's.

When I enter his room, however, I don't find her twisted in the sheets. His bed is still neatly made, which makes sense considering he slept with me. I'll parse over that glaring lack of judgment later. For now, I set my sights on the one task I should have been fixated on from the very start.

Finding answers.

I inspect the closet first, retracing my steps to the same duffle where I found the vial of Lorazepam and the explicit photos. Do I believe him when he claims to have never touched her? Of course not, though it doesn't matter now.

The side pocket is empty, the photos gone.

Of course, he wouldn't leave me with anything more than the breadcrumbs he deems worthy of taunting me with. I know this entire search is in vain, but I can't stop myself from scanning every shelf, inspecting them in more detail.

The clothing stands out to me, the more I inspect each garment. In fact, the female clothing outnumbers his. I'd be tempted to suspect he has some sort of secret fetish for wearing it himself, if the sizing wasn't skewed so small that I doubt he could fit a single thigh where the waist is meant to go.

Something I heard him say comes back to me, uttered in a tone so gruff and deep that I suck in a breath just reliving it.

I've obsessed over this body, Ada-Maria. What I would have you wear when you were mine.

I'd almost believe it... That he bought these with me in mind, my body, his tastes. If it weren't for the glaring fact that Alexi is the exact same size, along with most of the women in Terra Rodea. How many has he plied and captured before sending to Jaguar?

I let the resentment build, giving me the strength to keep searching, hunting for anything out of place, merely out of pure spite. I rummage sloppily through the hangers so that he'll know I was here, touching his clothing. His shirts. His pants. I toy with the material, noting its quality but also how new it all seems. Which makes sense—after dropping the Domino persona, he would need all new clothing with which to embody his freed self. A man who harbors more secrets than any man should have the right to.

And every step of the way, he'll only feed me pieces at a time, at his discretion. He must get off on my confusion, more than even my pain. I bet it makes him feel powerful to exert so much control over me, thinking he can anticipate my every move.

And if I were a smug bastard like him, I'd gloat over my captive's supposed innocence. I'd take joy in hiding snippets of information right under her nose, and I would relish in watching her squirm.

Whether by accident or subconsciously. I'm near that black duffle again. This time, I unzip the main compartment, even though it was empty initially when I first found the things he planted for me.

This time, it's not.

Inside is a neatly folded set of clothes. A passport. A wad of coiled cash. Underwear—*women's* underwear…

The clothing, too—a black sweater and light wash jeans— are far too small to fit Domino Valenciaga. Could they be Alexi's?

I bring the bag to the watch cabinet and remove each item one by one. The first observation that takes my breath away is, when I open the passport, Alexi's picture isn't the one I find inside.

Though, the name reads Alicia Garcia, I vaguely recognize the woman in the stern-faced passport photo. Her hair is a dark brown, the same length as mine, her eyes listed as gray, her height listed as five foot, five inches…

She looks like me. The photo could be one of me, in fact, though altered with darker hair. When I eye the clothing again, a dull sense of dread begins to build in my gut. While the right size to fit Alexi, they'd also fit me. The style is much more practical than a flimsy, revealing dress should I decide to go "wandering in the desert again," as Domino taunted. Or for another reason entirely.

Like maybe he plans to let me go. Take me back to Terra Rodea and refuse to sell me after all? Hope is an insidious impulse, flaring before I can counter it.

A more likely explanation is that this is what he plans on shipping me off to Jaguar wearing. Why not make his job easier?

Angrily, I tug my dress over my head and throw it to the floor before pulling on the sweater and jeans. I take the passport and stuff it into one pocket, sliding the wad of cash into the other.

Now I'm truly ready to play my role—a toy to be bought and sold.

CHAPTER EIGHTEEN

I exit the closet and eye myself in the mirror, trying to use this act of disobedience to distract from the growing fear, warning that, despite all of Domino's taunts about Jaguar, I still have no idea what to expect. The only name I have to go on is *La Guarida Del Tigre*—a place filled with men even more despicable than he is, I assume. Hell.

By the time I finally leave and reenter the hall, my shoulders slump with the weight of the impending visit. Jaguar's arrival feels more like an execution date, when I'll finally find out my sentence. Death? Or something far worse?

In a daze, I make my way into the white room and stare from the windows watching the day slowly slip away as the sunlight darkens, turning golden. I don't know what causes it—this imperceptible tensing of my muscles and a quickening of my heartbeat. A part of me is on alert even before I hear the telltale thud of a door opening and closing and a raised, masculine voice ring out.

When soft, shuffling footsteps approach my door, I'm already lurching to my feet just as Ines appears in the doorway, her head bowed.

"Mr. Jaguar is here, Miss," she says softly. "He requests that you join him on the terrace."

I notice that she doesn't mention one other figure by name, and I can't suppress the urge to ask, "And… Domino?"

She shakes her head, but if I'm not mistaken, a hint of alarm flits across her brown eyes before disappearing just as quickly. "Mr. Domino is not back," she says.

But I sense there's so much more lurking behind those ominous words. That gnawing unease chills me to the core as I stand and make my way through the house, bathed in the ochre light of sunset.

I hear him before I see him, a man with a booming voice that echoes loudly from the direction of the terrace.

"…So I came a little early," he says, presumably into a phone given that I don't hear anyone reply. "Don't worry, I'm sure your little birdy tipped you off the second she saw me coming. Just take your time out on your little errand, Dom-Dom. I'm in no rush. In fact, it looks like I'll just have to find a way to entertain Ada-Maria all by myself. See ya when I see ya, little brother."

He's standing at the balcony, eyeing me with a wink from over his shoulder. When faced in the full light of day without the shadows of Domino's bedroom to obscure him, the man is imposingly tall, built seemingly from the same mold as his "little brother." Muscle strains against the back of his thin white tee shirt that he wears paired with jeans. The tattoo covering nearly the full length of his left arm is on stark display—a predatory feline with dark fur, crouched among jungle leaves. I can't help but notice that its hungry glare resembles that of the man spinning to face me, his lips parted in a sly, disarming grin.

"You must be, Ada-Maria." His brown eyes size me up with a sweeping glance, lingering over my breasts, barely visible beneath the sweater's relatively modest neckline. I'm already sweating, feeling the jeans cling to my legs uncomfortably. Perhaps it wasn't so smart to try provoking Domino while having to face the brunt of the sweltering sun.

At the same time, some vain part of me is grateful for the extra fabric as a barrier against Jaguar's scrutiny.

He has an aura so different from Domino's—an all-encompassing swagger that instantly transforms this remote domain from an isolated paradise into a realm firmly under his control. He holds himself as though he owns the place, snapping his fingers to command Ines, who appears on cue.

"Bring us some wine," he says, dismissing her with a wave of his hand. "The good stuff. I know little Dom-Dom wouldn't want to be stingy when it comes to serving his guests."

As she retreats, his piercing eyes return to me, his smile even wider. "Shall we?"

He inclines his head, beckoning me to follow him to the terrace's second level. There, a familiar blond lounges on one of the white couches wearing a black string bikini. Her gaze is unreadable as she watches our approach, but when she turns to face Jaguar, I note that the angle is far different from how she'd contort herself before Domino.

She's not letting her breasts spill out, but bearing her throat in a gesture of subtle submission. My mother looked at my father the same way. Like she'd die for him.

And at the same time…

Like he had a knife to her throat, ready to slice should her expression convey anything different. I learned in my early childhood that slender line between love and devotion. And oppression.

"Baby, why don't you take a walk around the property. I need to talk to Miss Ada-Maria alone."

Alexi's simpering smirk falls flat. "But you just got here—"

"What the hell did I say?" His inflection never changed; merely his expression did. A hardness set into his mouth, and his eyes seem even darker.

Without another word, Alexi lurches to her feet and takes off toward the gardens.

"Have a seat, Ada." Jaguar claims Alexi's former couch, sprawling out with his arms braced along the top of the chair on either side. He nods toward the space beside him.

Instead, I pivot and take the couch across from him. His eyes narrow to slits, but his smile doesn't budge, remaining a fixture on his face even as his gaze takes on a more calculating focus.

"I think I prefer you naked," he remarks with a bluntness that sets my cheeks on fire. He eyes my chest with open disapproval and sighs. "Dom-Dom must prefer to keep you covered while he's away. What a damn shame. When we get you to the *Guarida,* that will change, I can tell you that."

"The *Guarida*." The word tastes heavy on my tongue, lacking the musical quality his accent gives it. "Is that where…"

I find that I can't finish that sentence out loud. *Where I've been sold to.*

"It seems our little Dom-Dom has been more forthcoming with you than he's led on." He leans forward, stroking his fingers through my hair without warning. It takes everything I have in me not to flinch, submitting to his coarse touch. "All for the better, though. I don't enjoy breaking in the new girls myself, but I'm up for a challenge. I'll give you a little crash course, even. The *Guarida* is my paradise, you see. A world where the trappings of society and the silly rules some stuffy men in suits decide for us cease to matter. It is freedom."

He runs his fingers along the underside of my chin, raising goosebumps. A part of me reacts to his touch in a way I've never responded to anyone—not even Domino. It's electric. The closest feeling I can compare it to is what I felt around my father's guard dogs. Rumor had it that he trained them with live animals, and they were always on a hair-trigger, taught to heed only his command.

Jaguar has that same look in his eye. Like all he wants to do is bite. Attack. Brutalize.

Only I doubt he'd heed any other man's commands to stop.

"You are very beautiful," he tells me. "I'll give Domino that much." He sits back and gestures toward his lap with a wave of his hand. "We should get to know each other more. Come sit with me."

It's not a request. Knowledge of that spurs me to my feet despite every warning blaring at the back of my mind to put as much distance between us as possible. I aim to play it safe, meaning to perch myself on the very edge of his couch.

He snags my wrist before I can, dragging me toward him. His smile remains as he wrenches me down, and he doesn't stop until I trip and land almost entirely on his lap.

"There. This is much better." He hooks his fingers around my ass, yanking me forward so that I'm straddling him, much like I did Domino not too long ago.

But this position feels nothing like that. There's no fragile familiarity, despite the animosity between us. With Jaguar, I'm on edge, painfully aware of the strength coiled in the muscle flexing against me.

"I can't wait until we become more acquainted," he murmurs, his gaze on my lips.

Maybe it's because I'm pathetic enough to admit that I wanted Domino for years before he took me. I fantasized about every inch of his body, and a part of me will always fight that attraction.

But with Jaguar…

My body can't get past the danger radiating off him in waves. It takes me a moment to identify it, but I stiffen the second I do—rage. It's far different from the lethal anger that explodes from Domino, barely restrained. Jaguar's hostility is far more nuanced, lurking beneath the planes of this handsome face, smoldering behind the dark irises.

"You have sexy fucking eyes," he says with an intensity that makes me jump. I've been so focused on observing him, that I didn't pay much notice to the fact that he's been doing the same to me. "Like you're thinking hard. I like that." He grazes my cheek with the pad of his thumb, brushing the hair from my face. "Plenty of men will pay extra to enjoy a girl who seems like she has a brain in her head while she's sucking his cock."

I grit my teeth, feeling my cheeks flame as I look away at the sun sinking into the horizon. Domino wasn't coy about this place and what would happen to me there, but still…

It's one thing to hear him taunt me like it's a game. It's another thing entirely to listen to a man state it so plainly. He's not exaggerating to manipulate me to conform to his twisted plans. He's being honest, and I think I should be grateful for that.

No more mind games to navigate.

Just a minefield.

"I'm surprised he told you," Jaguar muses, still petting me with the tips of his fingers. "Our little Dom-Dom never sent me a girl before."

He chuckles when I flinch and cups my jaw, guiding me to face him.

"Oh yes," he says, frowning. "You're his very first. Domino has always looked down on my little enterprise, you see. Acted as though he was too good to care for the girls, and guide them toward a better life. Until you, Ada-Maria Pavalos. Though it sure as hell seems that he got his money's worth out of you, first."

He strokes the edge of a scabbed cut on my forehead disapprovingly.

"Though if you could please a stuck-up, prudish motherfucker like little Dom-Dom, then you must be worth every fucking penny."

He slides his free hand beneath my sweater, ghosting the flat of my belly.

Given the number of unwanted touches I've had to endure from various men throughout my life, he should be no different. It should be easy to simper and smile and arch into his calloused palm the way I have so many times before.

I jerk back instead, nearly falling off his lap entirely. Domino's voice explodes in my head, grated and guttural— *I'll rip you to pieces if you even let him look at your body.*

It's instinctive. I can't help it.

But Jaguar's eyes gleam as he withdraws his hand, and I sense that I've made a terrible mistake. My first impulse is to relax against him, forcing my muscles to contort. Then speak, anything to distract him.

"H-How… How do you know Domino?"

His frown deepens. "He hasn't trained you," he remarks softly as if he's speaking to himself more than me. He strokes his hand along my cheek again, and I sense whatever irritation my reaction aroused in him diminish slightly. "At least the bastard did one thing right," he says. "He saved the best part for me. I should teach you the basics now, baby." His thumb finds my lips, grazing the seam between them. "You don't speak unless I give you permission. Understood?"

I swallow hard, but he must mistake the jerking motion for a nod because he chuckles and leans back, his posture softening.

"But if it's about our little Dom-Dom, I'm an open book. Ask me what you want."

I hesitate, sensing a loaded weapon more than a kind gesture. He's testing me, probing in his own, cautious way —so different from Domino's doublespeak and intimidation tactics. Jaguar is far more predatory, patiently setting a trap in plain sight.

If only I knew what might trigger it.

"Don't be shy now," he scolds, batting my cheek with his knuckles. "I won't bite. For now."

The ominous feeling grows, but it's not like I have a better option. It takes me just a split second to weigh the risk.

No matter what Jaguar does, I have nothing left to lose.

"Who is he to you?" I ask him, making my voice as soft and non-threatening as I can.

The demureness must please him because he tilts his head thoughtfully and shrugs. "Dom-Dom is my brother," he says. "Family is important to me, you see. There is no stronger loyalty than blood ties. Nothing."

I choke down the urge to ask the most obvious question. Instead, I take another tack.

"You seem so different," I croak in what I hope passes for an amicable purr.

He laughs, flashing a mouth full of blindingly white teeth. "You're smart as well as sexy. You don't need to share a womb or have the same sire to be brothers," he says cryptically. "Those bonds lurk in pieces of us you can never erase. If I were to fuck you here and now, plant my seed in that sexy little body. My child would make you mine in a way you could never escape. *Both* of you would be my family. Forever and always."

His voice is musical enough that even the most horrific imagery lacks the necessary impact. Only the intensity of his gaze gives the boast the edge of a threat. A promise.

My heart is pounding so hard I can taste blood reverberating through my tongue. I feel like my chest will explode, but rather than arrange for medical attention, he'd just fuck me in the gaping hole. I can see the intention in him, so clearly, my entire body goes cold. Paralyzed.

Then he blinks, and his smile widens, displacing any hint of malice.

"You know, Ada-Maria, I will admit that I had you all wrong. The way Dom-Dom spoke about you, I thought you were a dumb little cunt. He made you sound like a puppy on your daddy's tight leash—" he taps the tip of my nose playfully and chuckles. "I knew he always wanted to fuck you, though. Dom-Dom isn't subtle when he's being greedy. Selfish. I'm surprised he waited until recently. He *did*, didn't he?"

Whatever my expression must tell him makes him nod in agreement.

"He waited five long years to stick his cock in that tight little cunt. I think he's a… What's the word? Masochist? He gets off on control or some shit." He flattens his palm against my jawline, eyeing me more closely. "I was never as patient as he was. When I want something, I just take it. To be fair, most women want me just as quickly."

His grip tightens, urging me toward him, and I panic, blurting the first thing that comes to mind.

"Alexi. H-How do you know—"

I see stars and taste blood for real. When the world comes back into focus, I'm hunched over the cushions beside Jaguar, eyeing a strange series of red splotches speckling the white fabric. Then I press my hand to my lower lip and realize why.

He hit me.

"Remember, Ada," he says, almost gently. Like a teacher trying to enforce the rules of his classroom. "You speak only when I tell you to. I suggest you try to pick up on that rule quickly. We don't believe in second chances at the *Guarida*. You strive for excellence, but I see it now..." He grabs my chin, turning me back to him. I'm bleeding freely, not that he seems to care as the drops of scarlet drip down onto his shirt. "Those cucks are gonna bust a nut for a girl like you. Sassy and bold, but still obedient. None of that overly mouthy shit."

He means it, I realize with abject horror. To him, those vile terms are compliments. Virtues he prizes.

"I'm sure Dom-Dom has had plenty of fun with you. On second thought, I might keep you a little bit rougher around the edges than I typically like. I can see the appeal in it. And now I'm even more curious as to what other talents you might have. I heard from Lexi-Lex that Dom-Dom has a preference for bitches who give good head."

I fight to keep my expression clear. I honestly don't know if I fail or succeed, but somehow I manage not to hiss in disgust out loud. Does it hurt me that he lied so easily to my face—yet again?

Yes. God, yes, it does. It's a rusty knife stabbing through my chest, striking the one open wound on my psyche that Domino Valenciaga seems to enjoy poking. Vanity and jealousy.

He fucked Alexi. Or Jaguar seems to believe so.

"Hmmm." He makes the low sound in the back of his throat, drawing my attention to him. One look at his face, and I realize that once again, I've made a mistake.

If only I knew how.

"He's claimed you," Jaguar says, drawing out the word to convey a meaning that goes completely over my head. Something that surprises him. And irritates. His eyes gleam, turning inward as if he's processing some internal puzzle that's been on his mind for a while. Finally, he's able to solve it, but the resolution leaves him frowning, his brows furrowed. "He's told you that you were the only woman he's been fucking. Hasn't he?"

I blink, more confused than ever.

Somehow, Jaguar seems able to glean an answer, and he purses his lips, an eyebrow raised.

"Dom, Dom, Dom." His voice deepens with every iteration of the name, ending in a growl. "That's not very friendly, is it? Promising you to me and then wiping his dick all over you, marking his territory and planting dangerous lies inside that pretty little head. It makes me question his integrity, you see," he says, but his voice is raised, his anger palpable. "How can we have a fair trade if someone is already poisoning the merchandise? I've been good," he adds, stroking my cheek again, but he's rough, straining my tender lip until my eyes water. "I've upheld his little feud against Roy Pavalos. I've supplied him with my resources. I've kept our family business running in the background. By my fucking self, mind you, while Dom-Dom was off playing toy soldier and wiping your daddy's ass."

He grabs my throat, curling his fingers around my windpipe with just enough pressure so that I feel my flesh graze his palm with every breath I take.

"I always had his back," he continues, regaining his composure. Now he sounds eerily calm, almost monotone. The way Domino used to while carrying out my father's orders, no matter how heinous. "Always. Because family means something to me. Honor means something to me. Promises, Ada-Maria… They mean something to me. I wouldn't take for myself that which I already pledged to another man. It's just not fucking polite."

He's implying something. Something dealing with whatever issues lurk between him and Domino, but I can't keep up. Fear floods my veins slowly as the pain in my lip sets in. The cool casualness with which he uses violence shocks me, and I don't think part of my brain has still registered the blow. There's something impulsive and wild about his rage. He can smile while making someone bleed and never miss a beat.

"I always knew he had a soft spot for you, though," he muses, still smoothing back my hair, his expression contemplative. "The things we initially planned to do to you…" He chuckles darkly, and my breath catches in my throat. "But then little Dom-Dom kept changing his mind, always moving the goal post. I thought, at first, that he just wanted you for himself, but now I think I can see what he was really after. I can tell just by looking into your eyes, that you aren't like my Lexi-Lex—good for fucking, but not much else. No… I think you're a little smarter than that, Ada-Maria. Smart enough to know at least some of your daddy's secrets. And if I were a selfish bastard of a man, looking to betray his only family… I would desperately want to know those secrets." As he speaks, he lets his fingers crawl up to my scalp, sinking into my hair to graze the tender flesh beneath. Slowly, he starts to squeeze from both sides. "I have to wonder what lies our precious Dom-Dom has been putting into your head. Or what answers he's been trying to beat out of you—"

I think of Pia and his obsession with the past. Her body.

Jaguar grunts, letting his hands still. "You won't be a mean girl and try to keep anything from me, would you?" he wonders softly, his smile widening into a beautiful, chilling mask. "Because then we can't be friends if you deceive me, Ada-Maria. And that, you see, would be a damn fucking shame—" Abruptly, he cuts his eyes to something behind me, and his posture shifts, becoming defensive as he moves his hands to my waist, utilizing them like lead weights to keep me pinned against him. "It's about damn time," he snaps, and from the corner of my eye, I see Ines scramble to place a bottle of wine and two glasses on the low table behind me.

Jaguar snaps his fingers, his gaze cold. "Pour it." To me, he flashes another icy smile. "Ines here has served my family for decades. She practically raised my little brother and me modeling what I thought was the perfect example of loyalty and honor. But then, Ines made her choice. She chose against me, the man who saw her as family, the closest thing to a mother he ever knew." He speaks in such a level tone that the anger conveyed by those words is only visible in his eyes which glint more dangerously than before. "I suggest you think more carefully than dear Ines, Ada-Maria. I would very much like to be your friend—" Cutting his gaze back to the old woman, he snaps, "Leave us. Though, I'm sure you stalled long enough to ensure that your master is well on his way. I guess that doesn't leave myself and Miss Ada-Maria long to get acquainted, then."

He leans forward, jostling my body against his chest, to snatch a filled wine glass from the table. Rather than drink from it himself, he brings the rim to my mouth, and his expression loses all shred of feigned cheer. He's stern, inspecting me carefully. "Drink."

I don't hesitate, slurping right from the edge of the glass.

As I swallow, he stares me down so intently my heart races, my palms sweating. It's like he's waiting for something. A reaction?

When he's seemingly waited long enough, he sits back, satisfied.

"I hope you weren't fooled by Ines' subservient act. She's a wonderful actress, but she is no shrinking violet. In fact, I'm sure she's been filling our Dom-Dom's head with devious little ideas from the start. I wouldn't put poison past him —" He nods to the wine. "How he loves to spike drinks, I'm sure he's been drugging you while you've been here, dulling your senses to make you more susceptible to whatever he demands. We do the same at the *Guarida,* mind you," he adds, "but at least you'll be well accustomed to it."

It's getting harder to hide my disgust. The worst part is that he's right. All those times I woke up dazed, feeling high. I assumed he'd injected me somehow whenever I was asleep, but now I can see how he could have drugged my wine all along.

"Drink up," Jaguar commands, tilting the glass toward me again.

I have no choice but to take another sip, analyzing every drop that floods my tongue for a trace of anything out of the ordinary. All I taste is a damn fine vintage, and when he seems convinced that I'm not poisoned, Jaguar takes his own sip.

"Dom-Dom isn't like the rest of us," he continues, laughing softly. "He has a much higher tolerance to most benzos, opiates, and the like. It would take a hefty amount to down someone like him. I'm sure he told you all about his tragic backstory."

He waits as if prompting me to agree. When I don't, he laughs. "Well, it seems our little Dom-Dom is more shy than I would have thought. Especially with someone I would assume might be a kindred spirit."

Every muscle in my body goes rigid. Is this his way of hinting that he knows about my attempt to inject Domino with a taste of his own medicine? I can't tell if he's merely speaking to hear himself talk, or testing me purposefully to gauge my responses—and I don't dare ask him to clarify.

In the resulting silence, he takes another sip and sets the glass aside. Then he sighs.

"Alas, our private fun has been cut short," he says. "Though, now more than ever, I'm looking forward to seeing exactly what you have to offer. You'll make a fine addition to the club, isn't that right little brother?" He raises his voice, seemingly for the benefit of the figure who comes storming across the terrace from the direction of the house.

I turn just in time to see him reach our level of the terrace, dark hair flying out behind him, hands in fists.

CHAPTER NINETEEN

"Brother!" With a jovial laugh, Jaguar nudges me from his lap and raises his arms. "Nice of you to join us—"

"You show up unannounced, *twice*," Domino growls. His expression is iron, every single muscle rigid. Only his eyes reveal any emotion, flashing angrily. "I suggest you try not to make a habit of it. One might think that you didn't trust me, *brother*."

"And one might think that you've been having way too much fun with Miss Ada-Maria here."

As I scramble from the couch, Jaguar's hand flies up, smacking my ass. Hard.

I can't silence a gasp, but by the time it leaves my lips, my wrist is seized in an iron grip. Brutally, I'm wrenched to my feet and shoved behind Domino.

"Relax," Jaguar taunts, his smile unshaken. "We were just having a nice little conversation before you interrupted.

About the rules of my *Guarida* and what will be expected of her there."

"You hit her." He must spy the blood on Jaguar's shirt, because he turns, grabbing my jaw, tilting it for his inspection. His nostrils flare as he eyes my lip, and I can't even begin to process the reaction flitting across his gaze.

"I was teaching her," Jaguar corrects, his tone playful. "And I can tell that, despite as much as you've been fucking her, you haven't been training her much. It's a good thing, then, that I'm more than willing to take over from here."

Domino's brows knit together as he releases me. "I have until Tuesday," he says. "That gives me three more days."

"If I were feeling generous, that is," Jaguar says. In the blink of an eye, he transforms. Gone is the mocking grin as he lurches to his feet. Practically toe to toe with Domino, it's apparent that they're similar in height and bulk, but each man carries his strength in drastically different ways. Jaguar is lean, light on his feet, reminding me of his feline namesake, while Domino resembles a wall of stone, immovable and rigid.

"I think I'm done giving you more playtime," Jaguar adds, stroking his chin as his smile returns. "Yes… I think I'll take her back with me tonight and get well acquainted with Ada-Maria myself. Maybe I'll learn if it's her pussy or her mouth that has you so whipped. I'm willing to try both."

"Are you going back on your word, Julian?" Domino demands, his voice colder than I've ever heard it. I find myself instinctively inching back a step, and for a good reason.

At the sound of that name, Jaguar inclines his head, his lip quirking downward. "Anything I promised you beforehand is invalid," he says. "Considering that you've been lying to my fucking face from the very start. What have you told her, huh? And why are you so damn fixated on keeping her? It couldn't be because you're planning on taking her for yourself, right from under my nose?"

These past few days, I've become so accustomed to reading Domino's every nuanced expression, that I think it's the only reason why I catch the flicker of alarm that crosses his features.

Apparently, so does Jaguar because he laughs. "Don't look so surprised, Dom-Dom." Turning on his heel, he strolls for the balcony. "You may have your own network of spies and allies, but so do I. Some of the people who you think are in your corner have always been squarely in mine. I've known for months that you've been planning and squirreling away your money and assets where you think I won't see it. You've been clever," he admits, gripping the railing. "Very, very clever. But not clever enough. You see, Dom-Dom, you can't outsmart me. I am always one step ahead, and the next time I catch wind of you plotting behind my back, I'll come back here and run a knife through Ines' throat and use her blood to water your pretty little flowers. I fucking dare you to try me."

"You're bluffing." Domino scoffs as he barks out a laugh of his own. "Always taking shots in the fucking dark. Your paranoia will be your downfall, Julian. So eager to find a hint of betrayal. If you thought I was dealing behind your back, you wouldn't come here with open arms to sunbathe on the fucking terrace."

"You're right." Suddenly serious, Jaguar turns around, his eyes glinting with a calculating gleam. "I'd set this place on fire with you inside that pretty little house, and I'd use the screams of you, and all of your traitor staff, as the soundtrack to a nice barbeque I'd hold right here on your so-called terrace."

He doesn't look relieved of his suspicions. If anything, his raised eyebrow conveys irritation, as if he'd been confident of a win only to have his power play foiled.

Because, in this game of verbal poker, Domino has an unshakable poker face. I can't get a read on him either way, and I realize that all those years playing toady for my father paid off to his benefit. He's mastered the art of deflection.

Deep down, some sick part of me might be impressed before I remember that neither of these men has my best interest at heart. If anything, I sense that I'm some kind of toy being yanked back and forth between the two of them in a twisted game of tug of war. Who will win? I honestly can't decide which victor I prefer.

"Fine." Jaguar throws his hands into the air, his grin firmly in place once more. "You win. Why don't you tell Ines to find us something to eat, and we can discuss our differences like men, over dinner."

"Ines!" Without taking his eyes from Jaguar, Domino waits until the woman appears dutifully near the entrance to the house.

"Yes, sir?"

"Have cook prepare us some tapas and serve them in the dining room."

Jaguar claps as she scurries away. "Wonderful! After you."

"As you wish." Domino snatches my wrist before heading inside. I scramble to keep up with him, noting the slight changes to his appearance that I missed. He's wearing jeans—the first time I think I've seen him in such casual attire since he brought me here. His hair is windswept and wild, his shirt a plain gray tee shirt that betrays the tension coiled in his muscles. He looks…

Tired. Like he raced here, not expecting Jaguar to arrive so soon—a surprise I think the other planned for that very reason. He wanted to both unnerve him and catch him off guard. And he primarily wanted to speak to me alone.

I shudder at the potential reasons why, and decide to fixate on the only damn thing worth contemplating now. How the hell can I escape both men? Despite all of Domino's taunts about what awaits me in Jaguar's domain, meeting the man firsthand has cemented that I don't want to find out. My throbbing lip is warning enough—Jaguar's *Guarida* will make my time here, with him, seem like paradise and the thought of that utterly hollows me.

I go numb, reduced to staring blankly at the surface of the glass dining table as Domino shoves me into a seat beside him. Surprisingly, Jaguar takes one directly across from us without comment. Though I sense his gaze on me continuously, noting every little thing down to how many breaths I take.

Within minutes, Ines scrambles in, carrying a tray of tapas that she places on the table's center along with a fresh bottle of wine and more glasses.

I reach for one, desperate for something to dull the fear I'm barely able to keep at bay. My fingers have just grazed the goblet when I see a shift of movement in my peripheral vision. Domino. If I'm not mistaken, he shook his head. *Don't.*

"I don't think I'm very thirsty," Jaguar declares as I withdraw my hand.

If his refusal foils some plan of Domino's, I can't tell. His expression is more guarded than I can recall, even from his days at my father's side.

"Where is Alexi?" he asks. "I would have thought you'd want to spend your time getting reacquainted with her."

"Lexi-Lex, is taking a walk," Jaguar says dismissively. "Let's talk about Ada-Maria instead, shall we? As smooth a talker as you may be, Dom, I don't think you need three extra days. In fact, given the state of her, who knows if you'll lose control and render her unconscious for another week. I want her in the *Guarida* safe and sound tonight. If money is what you want, I'll pay whatever you think she's worth. If it's the sex you'll miss, I'll leave Lex here to satisfy any need you may have—bondage included."

"I don't think she'll like that very much," Domino counters.

Jaguar chuckles, shaking his head. "She'll like whatever the fuck I tell her to. Unlike you, I know how to handle my women. If I tell my Lex to walk, talk, and act like Ada-Maria here, I doubt you'll be able to tell the difference. Unless her sexy little pout isn't the *only* thing you want her for."

"You promised me three days," Domino repeats. "I want what I'm owed."

"And you promised me that I could have Ada-Maria Pavalos in exchange for my assistance arranging a hit—albeit a sloppy one—on Don Roy. Do you realize how precarious a position it places me in? To go against a man so revered in our circle? Many, many of my enemies might assume I'm vulnerable and see it as a time to strike."

"You wouldn't have done it if you didn't like the *position* it left you in," Domino replies, his head cocked, brows furrowed. "Right at the top of the pecking order. If anyone dares go against you now, they risk getting the same treatment. No one will take that risk."

"Not even you?" When his question is met with only silence, Jaguar sighs. "I don't like fighting with you, Dom-Dom. No two brothers should ever let something as trivial as pussy come in between them."

I stiffen when I realize he's referring to me. The sick part? I don't think he intends it as an insult. To him, that's all I am —a hole to be bought and sold.

But does Domino see me the same? God, I hate that I still can't get a read on him. I'm tempted to reach for the wine again and drain the whole bottle. My nerves are so scattered, my pulse racing. I feel my fingers twitch for my glass, but this time a firm, unmistakable pressure lands on my knee. His hand. The touch alone conveys his meaning —*do not drink.*

I let my hand fall to the table, and this time Jaguar tracks the movement, his eyes glittering with interest.

"I hate to pull the rank card on you, Dom-Dom," he says. "Really, I do. But I am the leader of the *Guarida*, and if I say I want her tonight, then I'm going to fucking take her tonight—"

"Fine." Domino pushes back from the table and shrugs. "Take her."

My blood runs cold at his tone, paired with his disinterested expression. He means it.

But Jaguar, on the other hand, doesn't seem satisfied. "I have to admit that I'm skeptical of your sudden change of heart," he admits, his voice grated with a rare hint of open annoyance. "You wouldn't be up to your old tricks, now would you."

"No. I just hate hearing my leader beg me for pussy," Domino replies. "Take the bitch. I think she'll like being put on display for the bastards at your little den."

Jaguar raises an eyebrow. "Who said anything about putting her on display? Oh no, Dom-Dom…" He strokes his chin, drinking me in with his gaze. "I think I might keep her for myself. At least until I discover what it is that has you so damn enamored."

The hand on my knee grips tighter. Too tight. Wincing, I try my best to smother the pain.

"I never thought you'd want my sloppy seconds," Domino says in a tone that's the polar opposite of the violence I feel in his clenching grasp. He sounds unbothered to the point of boredom, his eyebrow cocked to match Jaguar's open skepticism. "I always assumed that my tastes in women were far different than yours."

"Pussy is pussy," Jaguar snaps. "And what's 'sloppy' between brothers? Perhaps we can initiate little Ada-Maria into the family? Then I wouldn't have to worry about you always trying to slip away, so desperate to gain your… What do you call it? Your freedom?"

"We are *not* brothers," Domino says coldly, and his unfazed mask cracks—violently. His eyes flash, conveying raw, open hatred so intense that I stiffen in the face of it.

"Oh yes, we are," Jaguar counters, his smile equally feral. "In every way that matters, my friend. You belong to me. You are my family, and if some blond little bitch will make you act like it, then we both can take turns fucking her all you like. One big happy *familia*—"

"Enough." Abruptly, Domino lurches to his feet and slams both hands flat against the table. For a second, I truly think he'll lunge across it.

If he fears the same, Jaguar doesn't seem frightened. If anything, he looks… Excited. Like he'd love more than anything for the chance to fight. Destroy. Make someone else bleed.

"I…" My weak argument dies in my throat before I can even voice it, but the sound I make has both men turning to me.

Domino looks furious, his knuckles whitening as he clenches both of his hands into fists. Jaguar, however, laughs.

"Enough fighting," he says softly. "I think I have a better idea of how to end this. Let's let the little minx decide for herself where she would like to spend the next three days. Here, with you? Or with me?"

I'm not stupid. He's not asking as much as he's warning. All that talk of alliances and training. If I don't pick him now, as far as I know, I'm still destined to arrive at his *Guarida* within a few days. And I suspect that if I dared to choose against him, he'd make me utterly regret that decision.

In fact, he's such the obvious choice in terms of self-preservation that it's laughable to even consider choosing Domino. He's already sold me to Jaguar and made it clear that his interest in preserving my life extends only to finding Pia's body and whatever secrets regarding my father he thinks I know the answer to. Trusting him at all would be foolish. Stupid. I'd deserve the inevitable betrayal he'll commit against me, and I wouldn't even have the benefit of being surprised by it. The man has made it clear that he owes me no loyalty, and—after what he's done—I certainly don't owe him a damn thing.

Even his promise to protect me was coded in his trademark doublespeak.

But…

Therein lies the dilemma. Domino is a known evil. I have some experience, no matter how thin, navigating his moods. I've even learned how to manipulate him in my fragile, pathetic way, but it's more knowledge than I have against Jaguar.

He is an unknown entity and one that I suspect I won't be able to survive so easily.

CHAPTER TWENTY

"Since when do you let your women call the shots?" Domino remarks nastily, and I realize why—he knows the conclusion I've come to, and exactly who I'll pick. Hell, haven't I been taunting him with that very reality all this time? I'd gladly fuck any man who isn't him and beg for the pleasure.

"Now, now," Jaguar scolds. "There is a first time for everything. After all, it's rude to discuss business so openly in front of the merchandise. Let's let Ada-Maria choose for herself." He turns his gaze on me, softening his expression in a way that reminds me of a parent asking a naughty child which choice of punishment she'd prefer. A beating or a whipping?

It was a choice I was presented with often in my early life—and one I quickly learned to master. A beating left bruises and marks that could ache all over my body. A whipping, at least, would be regulated to my back, and the results of which would be far easier to hide.

"Would you like to come with me tonight, and meet your new friends at the *Guarida* three days early, or stay here with dear old Dom?"

Once I hear it stated out loud and so bluntly, I don't hesitate. "Domino."

The silence that falls is beyond unsettling. Like a bomb has gone off, ending one battle in a long-fought war decidedly. The losing side conceals his anger behind a cold grin, but even the victor looks shaken. Far from triumphant, Domino is left frowning, his confusion so blatant that I start to fear it can't be for show.

I chose wrong.

"Fine." Jaguar rises to his feet and snatches a cracker covered in some kind of sauce from the tray. "She's made her choice, and I am a man of my word after all. Let's shake on it." He pops the cracker into his mouth and extends his hand, but when Domino starts to reach for it, he shakes his head and nods to me. "This bargain was between Ada-Maria and me," he says. "I can swallow my pride and let bygones be bygones."

Warily, I place my palm in his, and his fingers latch onto my wrist as his eyes stare dead into mine.

"It's nice to see which sides we're all on."

He moves his hand as if he means to initiate a handshake, but the movement is too sharp. Lateral, not up and down.

I hear an unnatural crack first, and I start to incline my head for the source.

Then I feel it—*pain!* White-hot, it lances up my arm, and I'm screaming, doubling over with the force of it. My vision goes white. Everything sparkles, like some horrible, twisted high where my brain forgot to interpret the pleasure I should be feeling.

God, it hurts. Everything hurts.

And then, all at once, sensation returns to my fingertips. They're on fire, burning so intently I can't move them. They just flop onto the table as Jaguar releases me.

"Three days," he shouts, but the blood rushing through my ears distorts his voice, muting the ringing baritone as if I'm hearing him from underwater.

And someone else, who sounds louder, more insistent.

"Hold it to your chest," he commands. "Breathe in through your mouth. Breathe, Ada. I know it fucking hurts! Listen to me—"

"My wrist… My wrist…" It's all I can say over and over on a broken loop. I'm on the floor, sitting amid a pile of broken glass, clutching my right hand to my chest.

Jaguar broke my wrist.

Somehow I wind up in a different room, with a familiar marble floor pressed against my cheek and my right arm extended in the air, doused beneath a rush of cool liquid.

My brain can only process what happens beyond the agony in bits and pieces. One, someone is standing over me, holding my arm aloft, and at a slight angle so that it's extended over the tub, with my wrist beneath the faucet. My fingers hang limply, like a limb on a broken doll.

"That sick motherfucker." The voice is Domino's, and he repeats that assessment over and over, uttered with a different inflection each time.

That sick motherfucker, hissed with disgust.

That sick motherfucker... This time with an unsteady note in his voice I'm not used to hearing. Fear?

"When I get my hands on that sick motherfucker, I'll kill him." He means every word, voicing them with a clarity I haven't heard from him since I woke up on the floor of this damn mansion.

Gone is the mocking hate, and the twisted innuendo.

He wants to kill Jaguar with every fiber of his being. Very, very badly.

"Why?" I croak, though I'm not sure what exactly I'm referring to.

Why is he crouched beside me, holding my broken wrist beneath running cold water with a care that shocks what little sliver of my brain is still fully functioning?

Why would he sell me to a man like Jaguar in the first place?

Why does he hate me so much?

Why? Why?

"Ines!" His raised voice echoes off the walls, answered within a heartbeat.

"I'm here, sir."

"I think the bastard broke her whole damn arm. She needs something strong enough to get her through the night if we want to make it out of the valley in time."

The urgency he speaks with leaves me dazed. *The valley?*

"There is enough for a decent dose," Ines replies quietly. "But, you should know that this is the last of your supply."

"Are you sure?" The tension in Domino's voice calls to some part of me that stirs in response. He's worried. "Fuck. I was planning to get some more today, but that bastard came too early."

"Apart from whatever you have on you, this is it," Ines insists. "Do you really want to use it now? It could be hard to find more once you leave."

"Shit…" Domino clenches his jaw, and from this angle, he looks conflicted and so beautiful I hate him for it.

"Sir, you could go into withdrawal—"

"Give it to her," he snaps with a nod.

"Alright."

I sense someone approach me from the left, but when I try to turn to see who, Domino tugs on my arm, forcing me to lay on my side or risk aggravating my wrist. Only this position keeps the pain at bay enough for me to think.

And though I can't see Ines grab my left arm and wrench up the sleeve of my sweater, I certainly feel the needle she jabs into the muscle a second later.

I scream in shock, but the sting has already eased, and I recognize the throbbing ache working its way down my deltoid. She drugged me.

"Did you make the arrangements like we planned?" Domino asks next.

"Yes, sir," Ines replies, sounding more distant, as if she's speaking from the doorway. "But..."

"You've known me long enough not to play coy," Domino says in the closest tone to scolding I've heard him use with her. "Spit it out. What aren't you saying?"

"You should go tonight. He took the other one with him, but I know Julian. He'll be back. You should go now—"

"I haven't secured your passport yet," Domino says over her. "Mateo is fucking me on the timeline—"

"Don't worry about me." Ines' voice rings out with a strength I'd never expect. Jaguar alluded that she practically raised him, but that she chose Domino. What does that mean? "You go now. You won't get another chance. I know you prefer to stick to your plans, but Julian is like his father. They are unpredictable. That is what makes them so dangerous."

"You know what he'll do to you if he realizes beforehand," Domino says. He releases my arm, setting it beside me. Then he shuts the water off and pivots to face Ines. "I won't have your death on my conscience."

"So damn noble," Ines says disapprovingly. "That's why you were always at a disadvantage with him. You hesitate where he wouldn't. I know the risk after three decades of working with the Domingas family. Better than you, I think."

"I don't know how I can repay you—"

"Go," Ines says, but it sounds as though she's commanding him for once. "Find your answers. And I suggest you think long and hard about what it is you do value. Because Julian will take pleasure in destroying it before you can even admit to yourself that you wanted it in the first place." Her tone softens, returning to her dutiful murmur. "The arrangements are made. I'll have Miguel bring the car around."

"Luckily, Ada-Maria already made one part easier," Domino says, but his tone conveys more irritation than admiration.

Without warning, he lifts me into his arms, carrying me into the hall so swiftly I can't keep up. The next thing I'm aware of is that we're passing through the circular foyer. Then another door I've seldom traveled through.

Suddenly, we're in the dark night air, bathed in the sweltering heat. I strain to pay attention, noting the front of the house illuminated by windows flooded with golden light. The paved walkway. A car with its headlights blaring like the red eyes of a beast, eager to swallow me whole.

The drug is kicking in so damn quickly. Ines must have given me one hell of a dose. It's like I blink, and I'm seated, leaning against a pane of glass as the world rushes before me, dark and endless.

Domino sits beside me, bathed in the faint bluish glow of a dashboard, his hands on the steering wheel.

"Where?" I ask with the last amount of strength I have left.

His answer comes as my vision fades to black.

"I'm taking you back to Terra Rodea."

~ The story continues in Blood Bound ~

Hey there!

Thank you so much for reading! If you enjoyed the story, please leave a review and recommend the book to any friend you think would love this twisted world. You'd have my eternal gratitude. Even a short sentence goes a long way!

Then, come join the rest of us dark romance lovers in my Facebook Group where you can get snippets, sneak peeks of upcoming books and even help vote on aspects of future novels.

Come to the dark side:
https://www.facebook.com/groups/lanasbeautifulmonsters/

WANT MORE STUFF TO READ?
Join my newsletter and get a **free book**! Plus, you get to stay updated with any new releases, random giveaways and exclusive sneak peeks!
https://www.lanaskybooks.com/newsletter

Other Novels: https://lanaskybooks.com/

Lana Sky is a reclusive writer in the United States who spends most of her time daydreaming about complex male characters and parenting her Cockapoo Joey. She writes dark, twisted romance across several genres. Her titles include everything from mafia romance to vampires.

facebook.com/AuthorLanaSky

twitter.com/lanasky101

amazon.com/author/lanasky

pinterest.com/lanasky101

goodreads.com/lanasky

instagram.com/lanasky101

bookbub.com/authors/lana-sky